Though We Be Dead, Yet Our Day Will Come

by

Tito Perdue

Books by Tito Perdue

Lee (1991)
The New Austerities (1994)
Opportunities in Alabama Agriculture (1994)
The Sweet-Scented Manuscript (2004)
Fields of Asphodel (2007)
The Node (2011)
Morning Crafts (2013)
Reuben (2014)
The Builder: William's House I (2016)
The Churl: William's House II (2016)
The Engineer: William's House III (2016)
The Bachelor: William's House IV (2016)
Cynosura (2017)
Philip (2017)

Though We Be Dead, Yet Our Day Will Come

by

Tito Perdue

Standard American Publishing Company-
Brent, Alabama
2020

Cover image:
Pieter Bruegel the Elder, *The Peasant Wedding*, 1567
Kunsthistorisches Museum, Vienna

Cover design by Kevin Slaughter

Hardcover ISBN: 978-1-940933-40-5
Paperback ISBN: 978-1-940933-79-5

Frontispiece by Matthew Drake (see page 2)

"I have forever envied those who are most despised. I would have liked to murder a beloved human being and then to be seen grinning happily."—A. C. Foibus

CONTENTS

A PERSONAL NOTE

I'm obliged here to express my gratitude to those many who have had the patience, forbearance, and simple goodness to help uncover both of those slipshod misspellings that without their generous attention would likely have slimed their way into this rather hapless attempt to pass through the sieves of the big New York publishing houses where alone readerships of size may be profitably traduced.

One

I've waited almost too long to tell about this. There are certain types of people in this world, and I'm one of them, which is to say a pronouncedly archaic sort of individual of high principles usually seen in loose trousers, a short beard, and broad tie. More significantly, I have slowly over the years brought together enough funds to absolve me of social participation, of traffic jams, office buildings, and the sort of rote conversation that used to put me in danger of death from ennui alone. How much ennui was that? Just keep reading.

Two

To start at some remove from the actual beginning, I had hardly become resigned to life in the womb when I began to perceive footfalls in the hall and the sound of someone speaking. By the fifth month, I could hear still other noises that seemed to come either from a radio in another room or the outside world itself. And if once I had possessed perfect memory (memory of everything, the cosmos entire, planets, and etc.), these were being taken from me at a billion a minute as I drew ever nearer to this present condition where I now "stand" before you as it were (speaking figuratively of course).

I do often stand here in the midst of my northeastern room, a rectangular space cluttered all about with books, dark furniture, a saltwater aquarium, and other cultural equipment of various kinds. It gives me a view of the forty-acre patch of stubble currently being

contested between me and my unpleasant neighbor, a
soybean farmer whose own cultural equipment com-
prises a shotgun, a sullen wife, and a television set so
enormous that I hadn't needed to provide one for myself. He was and is a fool, or in other words a rich,
dangerous, and powerful individual full of stocks and
bonds and lawyers and the rest of that. Nevertheless, I
do believe I can still retain ownership of the land that
has been handed down to me. Or at least till Friday
comes around.

But probably you wish to know more than I care to
tell. In that case, let me say that over the last several
decades I've grown a good deal older than I had expected, older indeed than I ought to be or previously
ever was. Trapped as I am between seventy-six and
eighty-one years of age on this planet, and with eons
before that, I have more than enough to think about,
regret, and remember. An example might be 1950,
when I was remanded to a classroom in north-central
Alabama, a confined space spilling over with twelve-
year-old people who looked a lot like me. Seen in a
view from the sky (and assuming the roof were invisible), I can easily provide the biographies and current
locations of the some half-dozen individuals worth
mentioning. I shall actually do this a little later on,
once I have made a diagram and affixed it—I'll do it
now—to this page.*

Three

But today, I want to focus on Claire Wilders, who
henceforward shall be called "Claire Wilson" for pur-

---

* See frontispiece

poses of anonymity. She had been given a place in the second row, where the quieter and withal the more scholarly sort of girls had been apportioned. Bending scrupulously over their assignments, their noses almost touching their desks, it seemed they were carrying out the mandates of their pencils rather than the other way around. Of course, the script they made was oval and unworried, and so characteristic of the gender that it could have been the work of any one of them, reflecting as it did a shared psychology so unlike the genius and capacity for abstract thinking given to males like me.

I will add that the female coiffeur of that date (seen from behind) tended to plumb symmetrically on both sides of their tragic little necks, exposing a naïveté that must have been very concerning to their parents and well-wishers generally. Certainly *I* felt that way; how on earth would ever they be able to deal with the rough boys in the fourth row, not to mention the world at large and its many things? Me, I was in row number three.

Claire's neck was the most worrisome of all, a mere "stem," too thin, circumferentially speaking, for throat and vertebrae and the rest. Coming nearer, I could actually see where one of the little blue veins, branching from the carotid (itself rather small), was of the exact same color as the northern sky as portrayed in a certain Norwegian postage stamp of 1905 added recently to my collection. And yet that vein was pulsing with a force too weak to measure, or else was no longer in active service. But soon the capillary (for that's what it was) drove deeper into the milk-colored flesh and passed forever out of ken.

She was to grow up, Claire, to become a rather plain-looking woman who taught school, who was to have a good marriage (he expired), which she then followed up with a bad one that continued till this one also died. But perhaps I'm giving away the story some sixty-four years too early. For with *her*, as with us all, it's the details that matter most.

"Hi!" I said. (We were walking home after school, and I had had to run to catch up with her. She was wearing a blue dress with dots on it and a pair of matching shoes held in place with a strap, or two straps rather [one for each shoe], that seemed tinier than the task required. Each strap had three holes that were visible and a fourth that was always occupied by the little brass spike, about a quarter-inch in length, that composed the functioning element of the apparatus. She wore glasses, too, the frames matching [and not by coincidence!] the color of her dress, her eyes, her socks, and perhaps other items as well. I was only twelve that day, but already I knew that nothing was ever just by happenstance in the presentation of women and girls.)

"Hi," she said.

She moved about ten or fifteen percent more rapidly than was my wont, and I had to make an effort to keep up with her.

"How come you always walk so fast?" I respectfully inquired.

"Because!"

"Oh."

Me, I preferred to move slowly, sometimes even coming to a full stop when I drew abreast of a house with open curtains, or if I wished to hear what was being said on someone's radio. September it was, with just three hours before the proverbial stars would be falling on Alabama.

"I got an 'A' on the math test," I admitted.

"That's nice."

"What did you get?"

We turned at the corner of 10th and Highland and proceeded past Lester's house, where, owing to the evidence of the bicycle in the yard (the wheel still slowly turning), we concluded that the boy had reached this place only a minute or two before us. His father was known to be severe, a reputation somewhat alleviated by the vegetables and winter flowers the family maintained in their uncanny garden. I have seen gourds and parsnips there, also dormant honeysuckle and passion flowers (considered by the ignorant to be a form of weed) entwined in the, yes, white picket fence. Of Lester himself, he was a routine sort of person, and nothing further shall be said of him in this account. His nose was long and red, and we used to pull on it quite a lot.

Knowing that she would refuse, I hadn't offered to carry the girl's books, a clichéd gesture at the best of times. Not that I didn't have enough books of my own, which is not even to mention the little "suitcase" that contained my clarinet. Suddenly, I realized that I had put myself on the wrong side of the girl, where an errant car would kill her before it killed me.

Hers was a middle-class neighborhood in which the dwellings were neither too close together nor too far apart. In this district, I personally had three good friends and some half-dozen intermittent ones, and I was familiar with the floor plans of a not inconsiderable proportion of the homes hereabout. I had even seen inside Claire's bedroom, with its clothen giraffe and other childish matters.

If you have no interest in *my* home, you are courteously advised to return these pages to its 11½ x 8 inch manuscript box and go away. Truth is, I lived among my things in a narrow room with yellow curtains, or "sails," as I thought of them, that propelled the room in breezy weather. Already the sun had demonstrated an affinity for me—we're talking about late July and early August—and used to follow me home to take up a position on the floor. Stunned by summer, I passed the days harkening to the bees, faraway radios, dogs calling from the hills. History had already used up a great part of its tenure before arriving at last to this crescendo in the divine Alabama of September, October, and early November.

Four

I needed no floor plan to find my room. Situated where it was, I could have found it anywhere.

Sitting at my desk, I went back over the events of each day, pausing over certain behaviors of mine. It's a fine thing, to have a crowd of friends and never mind how exhausting it was to disguise my real self in order to enjoy the sweets of friendship. (For that's what it's like, ye who cannot know.) Those others, friends and enemies of mine, were more usually to be running about and throwing balls back and forth. Meantime, I had learned that the gutters held tiny bits of colored glass, some no larger than a grain of sand. You gather these up one by one, drop them in a jar, and hold the contents to the sun . . . You might say I have spent my whole life that way.

Later on, as I grew stronger, I was better equipped to follow my genuine calling, which was to draw apart to my mountaintop home and think thoughts that hadn't previously been attempted. Of course, I don't claim to have foreseen that eventual vocation, not at age twelve. Certainly not, not at that stage when what I primarily wanted was to defend my position as a moderately popular individual among my coevals. (On the other hand, I'm not absolutely able to distinguish between the me of 1950 and that person in his present iteration. The two have become interchangeable in my poor head.)

A good day, all in all, the Tuesday that followed hard upon. I had made off with a good night's sleep, some four or five hours by the clock, and had come out onto the porch with a glass of chocolate milk. The day was bright and sometimes windy, and I could see a red and yellow kite emanating from where Richard lived. That much-admired home had five (5) bedrooms, one of them a library and another with a piano in it. The kitchen, set off to the rear, was under command of a Negress of some fifteen stone dressed in an apron bearing images of yet other Negresses, also in aprons with Negresses on them. The dining room, meantime. had a very long and highly varnished table with eight upholstered chairs ranged up and down both sides. Always there were flowers, yellow roses most often, in a porcelain bowl.

I never knew how the family had come into such good circumstances, save that it had to do with an inheritance of some kind related to investments having to do with a whole raft of things. But it mustn't be imagined that Richard's father, charged with managing his own portfolio by the age of thirty-two, had been able to avoid a demanding life. He used to sit in that room of his and take telephone calls.

Richard himself went off to college, where I was not to see him again till the class reunion of 2014. Even after the years, his face, owing to the two little tufts of hair resembling horns, remained very like a snail's. The second-most intelligent boy in town, he was a mild and reasonable sort of type possessed of average size and weight. His parents were reasonable, too, neither too strict nor latitudinous, neither too fat nor yet too lean, and in short the most seldom-mentioned family in the valley. Him it was (the son, I meant to say) who now came strolling past my porch.

"Hi," we reciprocated.

"Where're you going?" the narrator asked.

"I don't know. You coming?"

The pavement extended only a short distance before turning into a dirt road that led past Geraldine's house, a two-bedroom affair with a sunroom off to one side and a mantelpiece that used to have mounted photographs on it. In memory of her, who had moved away to Texas, we slowed, saying nothing to the old woman watching suspiciously from the half-opened door. Really, was she supposed to be a decent exchange for the missing girl? Sadness came down over both us two boys.

In those days, it was but a short stroll to the downtown metropolis that over the past century had brought together some twenty thousand inhabitants sorted by gender. But mostly my eye was for the stores and movie theaters, and the good chance of meeting others of my own age and type. Together, we passed in and out of the Woolworth's with its staff of old women too experienced to let us out of their sight. I took note of a pocketknife with the image of a cobra on it. (Sixty-four years later, the knife was gone, and the store itself had turned into a tattoo parlor, a suntan salon, and a federal agency of some description.) Richard had meanwhile focused upon a manikin in a black brassiere. He was even worse than me in that respect.

"I'm going to have me a wife like that," he decided. "Someday."

"I doubt it."

"And I'm going to make her wear stuff like that, too. All day long."

He had a point. She had a spiritual face, did the woman, and seemed to be gazing up at something on the ceiling, something exceptionally good. "Boy howdy, I bet she could . . ."

I stopped him. We were being watched by an elderly woman with blue hair and a face that had much to do with her overall personal presentation, the same old woman who just a week or two earlier had shooed me from the shop altogether and into the road.

"We ain't doing nothing wrong!" Richard called to her.

"Oh, good Lord. You don't have to *do* anything," I tried to explain. "They can tell just by looking."

The street scene had changed by the time we left the store. The sun was lower and had taken on a plangent quality. I saw all the old familiar buildings, the upper windows turned to amber in the afternoon light. The town was in suspension, as also the few remaining pedestrians frozen in mid-stride with one foot off the ground, a trick of the mind that enables me to stop the world whenever I want. I should have explained that *reality* (reality as understood by superior persons) is but a painted canvas designed to hold the interest of the electorate and keep it more or less tranquilized. You still don't know what I'm talking about of course.

We two boys continued forward, past where the town's worst people were sitting at the bar in the town's worst tavern. Fifteen faces turned to watch as Richard and I skipped past the open door. In the fullness of time, these people were to prove even worse than we had supposed, a congeries of kidnappers, addicts, poker players, and the sort. I recall one face in particular. And that from deep inside there came a Hank Williams song, one of the best of his whole *oeuvre*.

We met and then strode on past Billy Tate, a heavily tattooed twenty-year-old ninth-grade Navy veteran whom no one in right mind wanted ever to irritate in any way whatever. We both, Richard and I, put on solemn expressions and kept our eyes directed straight ahead. A sudden onset, a delirium of harbored rage, and he might just as likely have turned upon us and have beaten us both to death with the same hands as had already slain some dozen Japanese.

"He's watching us!" my friend hissed.

"Be quiet!" We knew we couldn't have stood up to him, not even the two of us working in tandem. Therefore . . .

. . . we went on, crossing over into a domain of divine smells escaping from the bakery. The baker himself, a remorseless man, had actually set up a fan to force those scents out into the city where they had an effect upon people. I have seen grown men hurry into that shop and then come away four minutes later with little white paper sacks bearing frosted buns, *petits fours*, and gingerbread men. Richard might or might not have money in his pocket, whileas for me, I'd brought no funds at all.

"Got any money?" the boy asked. "You don't, do you?"

"Naw."

We entered anyway and viewed the wares. Never, not until I became much more prosperous, was I ever to have all the pastries I require. I waited to see if

Richard would do the right thing, and sixty-four years later I still remember his gift, a cinnamon roll with a depth of white frosting on it. I could have used twenty of them. That was when he took out a bill of specie— (it would be years before I myself possessed money in paper form)—took it out and passed it to the baker. This latter person was by no means any kind of normal Southerner, and instead of the jolly fat man he should have been, he was thin and highly atrabilious, and his supposed eyes could not be seen in the depths of his midnight head.

We left therefore, arriving two minutes later at the best place in town, an old-fashioned drugstore that smelt of sweets and medicines of all kinds. Here the pharmacist *was* as he should be, a serious individual, educated and bald, who stood attentively behind the counter at all hours of the day and night. No one knew how many births he had forestalled by means of the prophylactics kept behind the counter in a little drawer. Today the place was free of high school people, giving us access to the town's best table that sat adjacent to the window. Sooner or later, everyone in town would pass that way.

He possessed, Richard, a pocketknife, small but sharp, that he carried always. Now, lifting it from his pocket, he opened the larger blade but then put it back and opened the smaller one instead. A mathematical sort of person, he cut his pastry into eight little squares and then hefted them one by one to his mouth on the point of his knife. He chewed slowly and in rhythm, looking straight ahead to appraise each bite individually. He was a well-organized person, calm, intelligent, and cold.

Out on the sidewalk a black woman lumbered past, another 300-pound item too slovenly fully to lift her moccasins off the ground. A thousand years might go by, but never was I to concede to such people the right to live in my hometown. I wanted white people only, men in suits and boys as smart as me. Girls in colored sweaters, autumn leaves, and songs by Patti Page. Every boy his dog and each girl her cat.

A fastidious type, Richard finished off his pastry and then spent a minute folding and refolding his paper napkin. With nothing left to say, we focused on the window, the most interesting pane of glass in town. It allowed us silently to critique the multifarious townspeople moving past. As to Richard himself, I had long ago recognized in him my only possible competitor in terms of integrity, good grades, intellectual astuteness, and athletic incapacity, and would gladly have liked to know what was going on just then inside his head. A person like that, he might become a name in some abstruse field of knowledge. Or he might retreat into his parents' 4,250-square-foot home and cocoon himself in a fifty-year spell of unhurried thinking. Or go off to college where I wouldn't see him again till the class reunion of 2014.

Five

It's not as if several hundred pages are missing. Instead, I'm resuming this confession *sixty-four years later*, hoping to offer a "snapshot" of the decadence that has turned our country into what you see around you today, namely a historical embarrassment that causes people no longer to be afraid of death.

"Dr. Fredrickson, I presume," said I, coming up to my friend. All those years had gone by, and yet his face was as much as ever like a snail's, even to the horns. Just now he was conversing with a woman whom I ought to have recognized, and did.

"And Caitlin! Gosh, it's good to see you again."

She produced a smile, I guess it was, contorting her face in such a way as to bring out into the open a set of wrinkles that she couldn't have wanted me to see. During the long interval, she had developed a more dignified posture, and her appeal had improved to about average for her age and weight. She dwelled in San Francisco but was thinking of abandoning that area to more cutting-edge people.

"It just keeps getting bigger and bigger," she said, speaking of the city.

I waited for her smile to evaporate, whereon she smiled again. I had personally kissed that bitch a score of times in the old days; now she hadn't even the courtesy to shake my offered hand. Meantime, Richard had maneuvered to face me, giving me my first good sight of him since 1950. His presentation *was* relatively good, his apparel first class, and no doubt it was at his wife's persistence that he had an initialed handkerchief spilling from his upper left pocket.

"No, no," he claimed. "I picked this handkerchief myself. And besides, I'm divorced now."

"Ah. Well, that's probably best."

"Yes, I remember you now," he admitted. "You're the one we used to call Lee, right?"

"And you were right to call me that."

"Thought so. Say, you don't seem to have made out so well. Been sick or something?"

"Little bit," I lied. "You know how these things are."

"That's what I figured."

"Say, why don't we go over there, there behind the punch bowl where there used to be that lecture hall with the oriental drapes? I want to hear about your divorces, etc. And your amazing career!"

"My career," he said, "was not quite what you might have heard. You owe me fifteen cents, by the way. Or about fifty dollars, with interest."

We laughed. Fifty dollars was more than I had, and my credit had been rescinded three years earlier. I did have some money, that much was true, but didn't want to break a paper dollar into silver cash.

"But you're a millionaire, Richard! You don't need my fifteen cents for Christ's sakes!"

"I *used* to be a millionaire, you mean."

"Still are!"

"Possibly. Have you tried the punch? Not bad."

"Why, no. Bring me some, too, OK?"

(I had at one time wanted to be a millionaire, and to retire before the age of thirty. Unhappily, I had placed the better part of my capital in the sovereign debt of Somalia and the worse in a privately held airline company trying to get off the ground, so to speak.)

I had to wait for my punch. The miscreant had overfilled one of the glasses and on his return journey had spilled a share of it on someone's—couldn't remember her name—lovely gown. It *was* good, the punch, and soon we two were staring at each other through the disfiguring lens of the bottom of the two glasses.

"Hmm. Maybe we should have another," my friend mooted. (Was it my imagination, or had the alcohol already incarnadined his nose?)

"Yes. But try not to spill it, OK?"

Again, I had to wait for it. He had permitted himself to get in conversation with a lady in a pink dress who at first had appeared to be more or less normal.

Spying at her through the bottom of his tumbler, Richard seemed entranced by what she was saying. Meanwhile, he was sipping alternately at both his drink and mine. I had to go and take over into my own possession the glass with the cherry in it. We fought for it, though only briefly.

"Leland?"

"Who's asking?" I rejoined, looking back squarely at that same girl who in the old days had perhaps disliked me more than anyone. (I want to say that she disliked *me* more than anyone, not that her dislike was itself a stronger emotion than anyone else's. Hers had been a *manifold* dislike in other words, and I expected it to have persisted up to present times. However, she did appear to have softened in old age, and of course I no longer had to fear that she might report me to Miss Beasley.)

"I almost didn't recognize you!" she went on. "You look . . ."

"No, I'm fine. Just need to slow down a bit."

"Slow down from what?"

(She was doing it again.)

"Mental strain."

She laughed. "Yes, that always did cause you a lot of strain. You need to be more careful, Lee."

"Oh, I'm reasonably careful. At our age, we especially have to watch our calories, too, don't you agree? And all that cholesterol!"

"You think? At our age maybe it just doesn't matter anymore."

"Right. And for some people it never mattered anyway."

She reddened and then turned to look for Miss Beasley, who will have died many long years ago. I smiled, always a difficult exercise for me, and then turned my attention to yet another old person who used to be young, in this case the deplorable Willie Smits, now once again released on probation. Drunk already, he was standing alone, teetering in all directions. That was when I set eyes upon a developed woman only vaguely familiar to me.

"Jesus. Look at the lungs on that one," I remarked to Richard. I spoke quietly and only a very few could have heard.

"She's had a breast amplification."

"At age seventy-six!?!

"No, no. She had one side done in '71 and the other in '73. It was a lot more expensive in those days."

"Good Lord. I don't remember her at all."

"She used to be a man."

"Great Scott!" I spilt an inch from both my drinks.

"You're behind the times, Lee. How would you like to enrich yourself with a few kangaroo genes? It's been done."

"O brave new world! Who did she used to be? No, never mind; I really don't want to know."

"Sam."

"Great Scott! I used to go hiking and camping with that son-of-a-bitch!"

"Calls herself Samantha now."

"We've been hornswoggled. Get rid of her."

"*You* get rid of her."

I did try. With seeming indifference, I came up, circled three times about her personhood, and spoke:

"Sam!" I called. "Almost didn't recognize you."

"I can't imagine why. But you look just the same, Ricky."

"Lee, actually."

"Oh? Well then, you *don't* look just the same."

We both laughed long and thrillingly. I knew right well that I looked more the same than did she, who used to bench-press 225 pounds. That was when Richard felt he also needed to have a say:

"Right. She looks better now than when he . . . No, I mean . . ." He quieted. His drink was only about thirty percent finished and from the splotches on his cheek, I deduced that he'd not be having any more. We were in a crowd of smiling women, all of them in pastel makeup, all still locked in a beauty contest. I thought of Mycenaean Helen and the ploys *that* one must have tried at seventy-six. That was when the egregious Willie wandered up and tried to ensnare the rest of us in some sort of low-grade humor having to do with his favorite interests. His mouth was enormous as a crocodile's (or anyway an alligator's), but his teeth were gray and small, stunted, one must suppose, by their eternal immersion in tobacco smoke. It was 9:17 in the evening, not too early for me to gather my things and run back home to my woman, my books, and my dogs pining for me in occupied Georgia. Meantime, another person had come up and was loitering a few inches off to one side. I couldn't blame him. It's embarrassing to be alone in the midst of people pretending still to be good friends. Or colleagues, anyway. I shook with the person, who shook right back. A tall son-of-a-bitch with a goofy face, I assumed he had probably been a member of our famous basketball team.

"Hey!" I said. "I was afraid you hadn't come!"

"Yeah," he said. "I decided to come."

"And succeeded, too. Is your wife here?"

"Which one?"

"I see. Divorced then."

"I wanted to bring all of 'em, but Curtis said it waddn't allowed."

"The hound."

"Is this your wife, for example?" he asked, nudging the fat woman who had loathed me then and loathed me now.

"You kidding? No, no, my wife is a different type altogether."

"Thanks, Lee." She smiled wanly, and then turned and moved off in the direction of a clutter of women sharing photographs of grandbabies and vacations. Some of these people had been pretty, some had had personalities, while some seemed actually to have become better persons, which is to say more stately in address, more placid in facial expression, indeed almost *spiritual* in one or two cases. One case, anyway. With nothing now but men in my own circle, we began right away speaking of football and cars, of surgical procedures and one or two dirty jokes that I regret not having jotted down in the little notebook next to my shoulder holster. I would have preferred to be rid of Willie, save that his jokes were by some distance the best of all.

Just then an elderly man entered the room. Elderly man? He was no more elderly than me, for Christ's sakes—entered and began walking up close to people in order to identify them, as it seemed. He was in bad shape, too thin by much, exiguous hair, and a face that had been through several too many hailstorms.

"My God. That's not Lloyd, is it?" one of us (not me) asked. "Doesn't seem to have made out so well."

"Cancer."

"Yeah. And a lot shorter than he used to be. See how his trousers are all scrunched up?"

"I reckon your trousers would be like that, too, if you'd had the same kind of surgery as that pore bastard."

"He's looking at us."

"He might be looking at you, but he's not looking at me."

"Oh? I think you'll see that he is in fact looking straight at you."

"You're right."

I knew then that I'd probably be lighting up a cigarette real soon. It keeps a person busy and tends to allay his nervousness when among people who have in large part become strangers to him. Turning to my one true friend, I said:

"Look around, Richard; this is the last generation held together by race, language, and religion. All these ties must now be broken for the economy's sake. I see a new Dark Age of great wealth and perfect unhappiness."

"We're already there! I have great wealth, and look at me!"

In truth, he was a doleful sight, him with his divorces and spoilt offspring, a prototypical prototype of the New American Man. His monthly pharmaceutical bill would have foddered a whole village in normal times.

"Gosh, I really don't want to talk to that pore son-of-a-bitch," said I, referring to Lloyd, who continued to move in my direction with a jolly grin.

"It's not contagious, for God's sakes. Cancer."

"Oh, I see. So you think cancer is the only thing wrong with him? I tell you, Rich, there are more diseases in this world than are *dreamt of* in your little philosophy."

"Oh, I wouldn't go so far as that. My philosophy
has all kinds of diseases in it. Say, fetch me a drink,
would you? I want to get rid of this headache."

Appeared then a woman in the hall, a person in a
red gown wearing too much mascara and a tattoo on
her goiter. Hard to believe that a woman as old as that
could have opted to be as tawdry as this one categori-
cally was. I seemed to remember her as that good xy-
lophonist in the Junior Orchestra. She, too, was
someone I didn't want to talk to.

"She's looking at us."

"We can scatter, or we can talk to her. That's the
choice."

Lloyd scattered, but we others stood by with bright
golden smiles. She had done a lot of work on her dentition and yet her smile remained . . . How to say?
Disconcerting. I feared to kiss the woman's hand, lest
I injure myself on her encrusted ring.

"Hi!" I said, once I had gained possession of myself.
Observing us from afar, some half-dozen superannu-
ated dryads were tittering at the bar. Meantime, our
rented orchestra had just now started up with the
music of our special decade.

"Hi!" as I have already said I said. "You're that girl
who used to play the xylophone in Junior Band!"

"No, actually I just moved here."

"Ah. And so you never actually attended our school
at all. So why . . ."

"I'm the hostess. One of them."

"Hostess! Aren't we fancy? Don't want to fetch me
a drink, do you?"

She gave me a rueful look but then did turn and
toddle off to where the almost-empty punch bowl fea-
tured a final ice cube being piloted by a small green
fly. The creature couldn't have drunk very much,

however, not with its belly as extended as it already was.

It wasn't an "orchestra" we had hired, but rather a local combo fronted by a jigaboo with a pretty good voice. I had in my head a long list of songs I would have liked, ballads by Billy Eckstine, Patti Page, Tony Bennett, and other personalities of that immemorial age. I have hated all forms of cultural decay, most particularly when I compared the music of yesterday with the tribal chants of these waning days. It was just then I spotted Percy Shreck, previously the worst person in town, but now somewhat chastened, it appeared, by reason of the six years he had served in the state's most famous building.

"Dingo!" I said, extending my hand and then after ten seconds had gone by, taking it back. He hated his birth name—I had forgotten about that. "You remember me, don't you?"

"Sure. You were that guy, right?"

"Right!"

"When did *you* get out?"

His right arm was a prosthetic device, while on his composite finger he wore a massy ring that had grown into the unfeeling material. Worse still, he had incurred a wound that had missed his left eye by not much more than a really very small distance indeed.

Six

By 10:04 I required another drink and to that end had put myself just next to the table where two non-Caucasians were dispensing the stuff. Why was I not surprised that the bottles, the glasses, and the ice machine were as haphazardly disposed as they were? Enduring it as long as I could—I'm a fastidious type, always have been—I took the sponge and while exhibiting a serene expression began to swipe up the hundred-proof puddle that had actually spread to the edge of the table and was dropping over the side. The bottles, too, were arranged, or rather not arranged in any pattern, as if those items enjoyed that sort of close contact, each with another.

"We'll take care of that, sir," said the ranking bartender in the red jacket. He must have been six and a half feet tall and weighed even more, and could easily have reduced me to pulp had only he'd been willing to do what he wanted. I have seen Ethiopian faces in all sorts of places, mordant visages characteristic of Cenozoic days. Deep-set eyes, weak chin, etc. This man was not in the least like that.

I ordered a Tom Collins but declined to pay for it when I perceived Richard moving toward me from afar. He had done well, fetching me a drink with a cherry in it.

"Hi," I said.

"Damn, Lee; I been chasing you for the last quarter-hour!"

"Pay for my drink, will you? I don't have my wallet."

"I already paid for this one!" He pointed to the drink with the cherry in it, spilling a quantity of his own beverage as a by-product of that action. His face had darkened somewhat over the past fifteen minutes and looked like a drawing by a child, or as if copied from a Merovingian coin. His hair was oiled, save where he hadn't any. Consequently, I put both my drinks into service and by supping off each of them in turn, brought the level down to such an extent that I could unite both quantities into one glass alone. In the mid-distance, I then perceived a girl who used to be fat but now, in opposition to the current rage, was praiseworthily thin.

"How on earth," I asked, "did you do it?" That was when I realized that I must abbreviate the distance between us if I wanted to hear her, and she me.

"How on earth . . ." I started out.

"I heard you."

"How . . ."

"Well, I had enough willpower to get help. But mostly I'm worried about *you*. I just couldn't believe it."

I held up my hand to stop her. "Reading too much. Yea, and too much thinking, too."

"Sounds boring."

"Boring? We *never* get bored, people of my sort. It's your mediocrities who need outside stimulation. Or live far from libraries."

"Or live in little towns like this one. So full of gossip all the time."

"That's the best part! Faulkner, they say, used to wait for school to be out so's he could quiz the pupils on what their parents had been doing."

"And what *had* they been doing?"

"Read his books!"

She laughed. "But Lee, why didn't you bring your wife? Oh, oh, what did I just say? She's not dead, is she?"

"Dead! Hardly. Ha. No, she's as perfect today as when first I descried her in second grade."

"How you talk! Well why didn't you bring her with you then! I must see this perfect being."

"I wanted to. But her heart was set on *Othello*."

"Oh, Lee; you could have brought him along, too, for goodness' sakes! Nobody would even have noticed."

I smiled. Her head was like a grommet, or bezel, or like a quoit. Her neck, to speak of that, was highly reticulated and had submerged to an appreciable degree into her thorax. Neither I nor anyone else can say with precision whether life is tragic, or whether not, whether a comedy, or whether neither. She *was* funny looking, that much was as obvious as the work that had been carried out on her nose. Two minutes went by, both of us grinning back and forth and intermittently drinking in order to use the time. At last I said:

"Well! I think I'll go speak with Gloria."

"Yes, do."

I was glad to get away. Gloria, a more basic and man-worthy type, had seen me coming.

"Gloria!"

"Hi!"

"OK, tell me about yourself. Or the details, anyway."

"Well . . ." (She had been standing alone in the lower left quadrant of the auditorium just under the basketball net. It made her nervous to see a person like myself drawing nigh.) "Well, OK. I got married just out of school, but I expect you knew that already. Larry. He was so sweet in those days."

"Yes! He was the flute player, right?"

"No."

"Who used to be in trouble all the time? Remember when he brought his motorbike into the building and drove down the hall?"

"No, that was Robert. Anyway, we both had good jobs and we were doing real good—till the baby came."

"Too late now. How many others were there?"

"Babies?"

"No, husbands."

"Just two. But one of them died."

"Alcohol?"

"But he was getting better."

"No, this is just another typical twenty-first-century story you're giving me, Fay. But your third marriage was more successful I expect."

"That *was* my third marriage. I'm Gloria. Fay is dead."

"Just testing. I know who you are."

"Ignore him," Richard broke in. "He's about three-fourths drunk already."

"I've had maybe *one* drink. One!"

"Four. OK, that last one was mostly ice, I admit that."

"'Ice,' he calls it. Frozen alcohol in actual fact. Anyway, Fay wasn't the least bit like you."

"Damn, Lee," Richard broke in, "don't you even know the temperature ice requires? *I'm* the chemist here, not you."

"Physics. You were an undifferentiated physicist for Pete's sakes."

"Same thing, chemistry and physics. At their higher levels."

With that, I more or less gave up on him, this award-winning "scientist" who knew nothing of these special matters.

"Really, you ought to have studied *knowledge*. Like me," said me.

He laughed long and richly, gazing up to heaven as he tried to foist off onto me one of the two drinks he was carrying. He was a good person, however, if the truth must absolutely be told. We were all of us good persons, many of us, wherefore I lifted my vodka and drank. Good persons were we who had paid all sorts of penalties only to end up like this.

"He did as well as he could," Gloria continued, "and loved the children as much as if they were his own."

"I guess I've heard that particular bromide *ten thousand times*."

"And then the house got foreclosed. I lost my job, don't you see, and Billy had that wreck and couldn't work for the longest time. So we moved in with Billy's mother. She was . . . She had problems, too, don't you see, and we had all those children to worry about. This was in '64."

"Whew. She must be over a hundred by now. Go on."

"So Billy moved to Gadsden. He was making good money, but we didn't get to see each other but maybe once a month. He was saving up all he could and he was going to come back just as soon as he could. I was taking care of things. Of course I didn't know Timothy—he's my eldest—was smoking that stuff. He was having these *intestinal* problems, too, they call 'em."

"Go on."

"And then he met that girl."

"Timothy did?"

"No. No, Timothy doesn't want anything to do with those people. No, it was Billy. They had this girl working there, Cindy. She's . . . I don't even want to say it."

"What happened?"

"They're divorced now, Billy and her."

"We could have guessed it, Richard and I. What, does he want to come back now and take care of his responsibilities?"

"Not that I know of."

I said nothing. Having already introduced all sorts of nostalgic rubbish into my own preening conversations, I couldn't criticize anything she might wish to confess.

"Yes, but would you take him back? If he apologized, I mean? And if you thought he might go back to being a good husband again?"

She looked off into the distance.

"Oh, she'd take him back alright!" said a new woman who had joined our huddle. "And if she won't, I will."

Richard piped up: "Golly, you people seem to think you're still back in the '50s! You can't be carrying on when you're seventy-six! Just can't. Hell, you should be picking out your coffin about this time. I did."

He was right. I acknowledged that, at the same time accepting the drink this "scientist" had been carrying for my benefit. He wore an honorary ring bearing the intaglio of some Greek or Roman thinker who presumably had made some important additions to the wisdom of those days. By now we had attracted a mixed crowd of alumni who seemed relieved that at least a few of us had found something to talk about. There had been some danger that the invitees might all end up standing off by themselves with self-conscious expressions on their multifarious faces.

"Gosh, you've had a hard time of it, Gloria!" said one of the new girls. "I didn't realize. I'm so sorry."

"Oh, it hadn't been all that bad, not really. Not like Fay. Anyway I'm taking a correspondence course now. Bookkeeping. They got a new system."

I wanted to cry.

Seven

Gloria: she had come forth in the usual way, a bald-headed six-and-one-half pound baby female human creature with no conspicuous disabilities. Three days later she opened her eyes and looked for the first time into the face of her derelict mother.

Her mother had also come forth in the expected way, a six-and-one-quarter pound mostly bald-headed baby who soon left town in company with a shoe salesman in process of separating from his faithless wife. But that's another story, and although I have all sorts of free time in front of me, I decline to go into it at this time.

And so she was taken, was Gloria, by a neighbor who had two boys already, though she had wished for girls. Which is not to suggest that she proved any better for Gloria than for her boys. Working all day over a hot stove in a downtown cafeteria, she refused to believe that both her sons were striving in her absence to join with their five-year-old fostered sister. Or that the older had succeeded. Under those conditions, Gloria preferred to spend her time in the chicken house along with . . .

. . . chickens. Better she had attended school, if only her guardian had remembered to enroll her there. Already she was on the verge of failing capitalism's basic tests. Devoid of initiative, ignoring her health, fractured résumé, poorly tailored, how could she expect to get past the Human Resources Department of your midsize corporation with branches in South America? Really, could it even be said that she was American?

In normal times, she might have been a farmwife famous for her cooking. In times more normal still, her molester would be dangling from a tree limb with a noose about his neck. But not now, not today, not with her clothes, her rural accent, and her poor self-presentation in front of third-floor human resource departments. She simply didn't have the aplomb, to be absolutely frank about it. Her shoes were all wrong, and far from an accredited degree, she had never gone further than seventh grade in a school that did, however, have a good basketball team. Extracurricular activities? Don't make me laugh. And yet, she had been given *all the advantages* of the world's most advanced post-industrial society with more international heft than nearly any other address. One must reluctantly assume that she had no real wish for a successful career.

"Hey!" I said. "You've had three husbands, and Richard here, he's had three wives. We need to bring you people together, don't you think, and do some mixing and matching as it were."

"Shut up, Lee. God!"

"How many wives have *you* had?" someone asked me, a diminutive woman who looked like a tufted woodpecker with bright red hair.

"I shall finish my life with the same woman with whom I started. Even now, three hundred miles apart, we remain in each other's magnetic field."

"Well, aren't you something? We're impressed. When do we get to see her?"

"See her? You think I'd bring her to a place like this?"

We had been joined by others. They formed a crowd of the kind that might at any moment decide that I deserved to die.

"He's always been just a little bit too good for us," the woodpecker said. "Right, Lee?"

"*Little* bit, you said?"

"Yep, that sounds like Lee alright. Hit him."

Came again *Willie*, our generation's most questionable fellow. He never smiled, and tonight he was accompanied by what either was his wife, or daughter, or a transgenderite with a DNA identity badge affixed to his or her lapel.

"Who needs edication," Willie said, "when you got a nine-inch prick?"

"Nine-and-a-half," his partner amended.

Immediately all the better people moved away, leaving only the boys and the modified person. I had finished nine-tenths of my drink, but before sending Richard for another I, too, abandoned this crowd and went to join the girls conversing animatedly about prices, recipes, the death of friends, clothes, and other people's divorces. I had taken out my red notebook but after ten full minutes, heard nothing that needed to be written down. That was when I forced Gloria off to one side where a liveried Negro and a couple of Japs or mayhap Chinks—who has time to learn the difference?—were preparing the banquet table. All I wanted was a medium-done lamb chop to absorb the rum and let me be clearheaded once again.

"Gloria, Gloria," said I. "You remember the time we went to the movies and you let me kiss you several times?"

"No! Anyway, it was a long time ago."

"That's alright," said I. "I don't remember either. Now you've just told us about the early part of your life, but I want to hear the rest."

"What's the notebook for?"

"Never mind that. Tell me, do you still see Larry from time to time? I mean after he'd been sleeping with someone else over a long period of time . . ."

"I'm old, Lee. You're old, too. So I don't know what you're talking about anymore."

"Sorry. But surely you do still see him from time to time? When you're out shopping or something like that?"

"Well, he used to visit the kids sometimes. Till I met Howie and we started, you know, going together."

"Howie?"

"Yeah."

"Was he a good person, Howie?"

"Why, yes. Pretty good. Before he died. He had that horrible disease."

"Cancer?"

"No, the other one."

"And your last husband?"

"He's still up yonder in Canada I imagine. I got the papers back around in 1982, or thereabouts."

I turned my gaze to the floor where two couples, each more exhibitionistic than the other, were dancing wildly. One of them, a fossil of the 1960s, had a gray ponytail and was dressed in a pair of odd-looking glasses that announced his political views. *J'avais envie de vomir.*

"Want to dance?" I asked the girl.

"I'd like to. But my knee"—she pointed to it—"is pretty well played-out. Now *this* one"—she pointed to this one—"is still alright. You ought to of asked me way back then."

She was right about that, and I wish I had.

"*I* danced with her," said Willie brightly. "If you know what I mean."

He had done nothing of the sort, or so I hoped. I parted from him then and began to edge toward the banquet table where a great many good-smelling

things were being set out by the women. I came clos-
er, as did also our former flute player and her quon-
dam boyfriend. They seemed to be thinking of getting
back together again, those two. Of course she was not
nearly as pretty as she had been, while as for her
swain, best the less were said.

I had been smoking diligently, hoping by that
method to defray my appetite. The women had gone
the length of preparing a full gross or more of medium-done lamb chops together with baked apples with
cloves sticking in them. I had identified the chop that
ought be mine and had sketched a picture of it in the
little red notebook where normally I store quotations,
addresses, telephone numbers, and bibliographic de-
scriptions. That was the moment the female vocalist,
a black one the color of ink, stepped to the stage and
began a popular song from the 1970s. She was lithe
and had a bright smile, and compared and contrasted
excellently—I admit it—with her purple gown. Is it
possible that this race of people is so good with sports
and murder, with reproduction, drugs, and song, that
they must be tolerated in spite of all? I had hoped for
music from the 1950s, and right away the lady, who
understood what we were thinking, ensued upon
some of the romantic ballads of long ago, plangent
music, nostalgic and good, lethal for people of my
kind.

Eight

We were called to mess by a little silver bell. Hun-
gry people we were, judging by how each several
alumnus at once directed him- or herself toward the
swayback tables burdened with nutrients and flowers.

All save Lloyd, too drunk by this time to rise from the uncommonly comfortable leather-sheathed couch that lay over against the brick-made hearth that itself contained a goodly fire made of pinecones and sweet gum balls.

I had wanted to sit between Hester and Gwen, two of the nicest girls of 1950; instead, at the last moment, I was shoehorned in between the uncivilized Willie and another fellow whom I remembered just as unfavorably. One last consolation came my way when on that instant I discerned Delores, or her granddaughter possibly, seated directly across from me. I had been warned about her facelifts but wasn't prepared to find her looking as if she were about fifteen.

"Hello," said I, using that expression.

"Lee?" (Her voice was older than her face.)

"Yes! You flatter me."

"How so?"

"By recognizing me!"

"That's a compliment?"

Save but for me, everyone within a certain circumference laughed long, loud, and jubilantly. She said then:

"It was my husband made me do it."

"I see! But what are we actually talking about just now?"

"Why, my facelift of course."

"Ah! But no voicelift to go with it? No really, I think maybe I ought to have the same procedure."

"Have ten!" said Richard, whom I had thought was out of range.

"Yeah! Have a bunch of 'em! Sheet mon, you needs 'em. You feel me?"

Never had I heard such effrontery from a Mandingo-American waiter. I wished for someone to rescue me, someone white and plausible and with social legitimacy; instead, it was only Natalie who defended me at last.

"Aw, he's not so bad."

I waited as she came around and, after choosing the proper fork, tried to force-feed me my first bite of salad, a hurly-burly of artichoke hearts, avocado halves, cubes of yellow cheese, and the normal lettuce. Laughter. Me, too, I had to laugh as well, I admit that. The wench had brought both her present and former husbands, one of them fat and the others lean, one of them smiling and two of them wearing a tragic mien. The Mandingo had meanwhile traveled to the other table and had seated himself among the dismayed Americans. He had, of course, been hired to behave that way.

Me, I drank, setting up a pleasant reaction between the rum of ten minutes ago and the vodka now. It still needed an hour or so before my wife would be hearing the best of her opera, portentous music regarding the murder of a woman very like herself.

"She can't resist Verdi, if you know what I mean," said I to Willie, who had a tad of toilet paper where he had wounded himself shaving. His hair was short and sparse, like an orchard in which a great many of the trees had fallen over. And yet each separate strand had a girth more proper to a carbon filament inside a pencil.

"Whatever."

"Would you pass the asparagus please?"

"Busy. Get Nat" (Natalie) "to bring it to you."

The benediction hadn't yet been given, but already my friends were eating vigorously. I waited for the lamb chops, falling into despond when I perceived one of the supernumeraries absconding with my chosen one. A billion years might go by before I'd have another shot at it, assuming Nietzsche correct about the eternal recurrence of high school reunions. Meanwhile, I had lost my hearing. These things happen sometimes when I'm banqueting and thinking, and it's raining at the same time. In the silence that followed, it was as if we were carrying on a formal ceremony at the bottom of the sea. His lips, my tablemate's, were forming words, though it wasn't likely anyone could hear them.

We were offered an extended benediction by a rubicund man in a suede suit. He had gotten certain lines of Thomas Browne's mixed up with scripture, but when I tried to tell Hester, she replied like this:

"You always speak with your mouth full?"

I was incensed. "No," I retorted wittily.

She turned away. My popularity with her had always been at low ebb, and anyway she'd never been anywhere near as smart as she'd been credited. One look at her husband revealed everything one immediately needed to know about her and all these provincial types in general, a low-hanging bourgeoisie devoid of arts and languages.

On the other hand, the rain was slowly and slowly turning into one of the best that I had seen in ages. Starting out as not much more than a drizzle, it had become so vehement that a person's eyebeams could by no means penetrate this "curtain" (I call it) for more than a few inches. Drawing near, I was, however, able to analyze at close range the explosions of raindrops on a glass windowpane.

"Lee?"

I came to attention. By now, some of the more easily satisfied people had pushed back from the table, turning away from the various kinds of pies and cakes on offer, and so leaving all the more for me. To begin, I volunteered for a mint pie in a crenulated crust. Not quite so good as I had expected, I nevertheless made no comment about it. Instead, I reached for a bowl of ordinary ice cream, having to fight for it against the resistance of the black comedian whose face closely resembled those as had rendered Easter Island so famous. Next, I took up a pastry of one of my favorite types, a highly confectionary product full of splendid contents.

The storm was continuing, but the best was still to come. Of all the things that I'm not afraid of, storms rank near the top. I wanted a drink and had just barely managed to get it before all the lights went out, and darkness fell on Alabama. But instead of your ordinary sticks of jagged lightning, we were being given *exploding spheres* as round as basketballs that gave off a plethora of bright golden sparks followed by disgusting noises. We tended to bunch together, we old ones, as if it had been decided that we were all to die that very night. I could see husbands and wives, unified couples who would have qualified for the dual number in Attic Greek, could see them drawing apart from the crowd in favor of the dark corners (there were only four of these) there to await the end of time.

Me, I chose this interlude to attend the restroom. The lightning flashes lit me to the toilet, an unsteady artifact equipped like an old-fashioned sewing machine with a treadle that was hard to turn. I do abominate humanity's humiliating excretory system, as interfused as it is with the functions of romance. Clearly, we are not gods quite yet.

I returned to my favorite window, where almost at once some heavy person blundered into me with curses and noise. I have already said how dark it was.

"Jesus!" I submitted.

"That you, Edwin?"

"No, no. 'Edwin'? I sincerely hope not!" I palpated his face, or in your language "felt of it," right away coming upon that unusual nose that we used to pull upon. Shaped like a limp penis, the bullies used to pull on it quite a lot.

"Lester?"

"Yes?"

"Where the hell you been these last sixty-four and a half years?"

"Oh, I see. You want to make it seem like we used to be real good friends. But we weren't."

"No. Say, did you ever marry that girl? Just asking."

"Actually, no. I tried but, you know, it's like she didn't want any part of me. That's her over there."

The silhouettes were far from dispositive. I could identify Richard's, but almost no one else's.

"The one with the . . . ?"

"No, Lord. That's the goddamn coffee pot, for Christ's sakes!"

"The one that looks like a hen?"

"Yeah. That's how she wears her hair now."

"Well then, whom *did* you end up marrying?"

"'Whom?' Sounds kind of snotty to me. Like if I was walking across the goddamn desert and somebody said 'whom,' I'd know he had to be a real snotty son-of-a-bitch."

"I did fly over the Syrian Desert once. When I was much younger."

"Well I reckon so! All of us was much younger. What, you figure you're a special case or something?"

"You're drunk."

"I am not. Inebriated maybe."

"What are you drinking?"

"Drinking? No, I just like to go around holding this goddamn little glass way out in front of me. 'Drinking,' he says. Shit, Lemond, you're not any better than what you used to be!"

I tried to move away and might have succeeded but for the wall and approximately fifty persons.

"So who *did* you end up marrying?"

"Shit, bro, I never married nobody at all."

"Oh."

"I would of married that bitch over yonder, but she didn't want any part of me."

"And so you spent the last sixty-three years chasing after her—do I have that right? No wonder you're an alcoholic."

"Yeah. Kind of funny, ain't it?"

"I'll say."

We laughed convulsively, both of us spitting up a fine spray of liquor and coffee that settled, much of it, on the window itself. The lights now came back on, though I was soon able with my Will to shut them off again.

Nine

"I used to take her to the movies," he told, starting off on a long narration that I didn't care to hear. "We used to hold hands, her and me. 'Course now in those days she'd hold hands with anybody."

"The slut." (I had to listen to him. Still a bachelor in 1969, he had taken umbrage at Communist activities and had volunteered for Vietnam, a patriotic action that had cost him one eye and the use of his pitching arm. Who would marry him now? Not the one he most desired. On the other hand, the rich men of America *had* given him a bag of peppermint candy together with a cost-free stay of three weeks in a mediocre hospital in Omaha. I was obliged to give attention to him therefore.)

"No, she was real pretty back then Lee. Still is!"

"You might get an argument about that."

"We'd go to the movies. The old Paramount Theater? We'd go see the Bowery Boys. You probably don't even remember them."

(But I did.) "And that's where you did all that hand-holding I imagine.'

He grinned evilly. "Sometimes."

"Continue please."

"Well, there was this one time. It was dark outside and raining real hard. No, I mean *real* hard."

"As hard as right now?"

"OK, maybe not that hard."

"Go on."

"So we ran on down to where they was building that J. C. Penney's place. Weren't nobody there."

"You went in."

"Yeah. They had some lumber in there where we could sit on it."

"You sat on it. And after a few minutes you went ahead and kissed her on the face."

"Yeah."

"And after that your life has been all downhill."

"Pretty much."

"All the whores of Vietnam notwithstanding. I may have to write a book about you someday. But are you sure it wasn't all just a pipe dream after all?"

Again, the lights strove to come back on, again I beat them down. Me, I had rather starve in semi-darkness than gorge in bright light.

"She kissed me back, too. Once."

"Well why don't we just go on over there right now and kiss her again? I'll hold her."

"Naw. Her husband would beat the shit out of me. I only got the one arm, don't you see."

"OK, I'll hold *him*, and you can kiss *her*."

"I believe you really would, wouldn't you? You always been one of my best friends Ed. I appreciate it, too. Here, take one of my cigarettes."

"You don't smoke, I thought you said."

"Yeah, but that don't mean *you* can't smoke."

Claire came up, who had become a far more sophisticated woman than in seventh grade. She was so modern now, so insouciant and whatnot that I had trouble to keep from vomiting. She accepted Lester's cigarette and then waited in her sleepy way for someone to ignite it.

"Actually, I didn't have anything to do with those whores," the veteran insisted.

Richard arrived, a beaker of whiskey in each hand. They had been affiliated at one time, Claire and he, and now stood looking each other up and down. In her heels she was nearly as tall as he, and in spite of her age her bosoms still rode "high in the saddle," to borrow a phrase from other contexts. She had improved with the years, or rather had declined more gradually than some of the others. Richard did have a match but was so perturbed by her sudden appearance that at first he positioned the flame too near her left gland. The light it provided was trivial but at the same time sufficient enough to let us view each other's imperfections, some of them. She was crinkled around the eyes and mouth, Claire was, a pattern that resembled fingerprints. Lester was even worse than that.

"OK," Lester said, reverting to Vietnam. "They may of been one or two of 'em. But what would you of done if *you'd* had to spend two years over there?"

"Read," I advised. "Become a better person."

"Is that all that matters to you?" (Claire.)

"No, I would have liked you to get better, too. BTW, there's still some ice cream in the kitchen."

"You're so snotty. But remember this: Americans don't like snotty people. It makes us feel bad."

I accepted the drink that Richard had been trying to foist off on me, but realized soon enough that it had not even a trace element of alcohol in it.

"Jesus, Rich! What *is* this, for example?"

"You've had too many already. So just drink it and be quiet about it."

"I could of saved a right smart of money, except for them whores," the veteran claimed.

"Want to dance?" Claire asked, addressing both of us three men. Someone had brought a recording of *Dancing in the Dark* and had saved it for just such a contingency. She tried to ensnare Richard, who relented finally. No one could say they looked like a couple of twelve-year-olds entranced by the voice of Mel Tormé. They looked to be fifteen at least.

"Shit, I would of danced with her."

"You can dance with her next year."

"Next year? Be dead by then."

"Not me."

"'Specially you. And it don't matter how many books you've read; you're going to be just as dead as the rest of us. Maybe more."

There was some truth in what he said, or at least in a long-term perspective. "Yes," said I, "but look at ole Zippy over there. Everybody thought he had died thirty years ago."

"Did! That's his cousin, what you're talking about over there."

"Can't be."

"Is."

Came then to our ears a song by Billy Eckstine, my favorite all-time Mandingo.

"Soon," I mooted, "there won't be a single good voice left in the whole country."

"Hate to hear that. Say, how come you won't let the lights come back on? I can't see squat."

"And if all good things become extinct, it'll be because of you. Or people of your type anyway."

"Hey! I don't have no 'type.' All I ever did was defend my country and be the best person I could be!"

"By Jove, I think you've put your finger on it. 'Best you could be.'"

"Hey, I'm getting a little bit pissed with you! I can always tell when that's starting to happen."

I left him. There were but three couples still dancing, and even those were showing signs of depletion. I struck a match, hoping to locate Richard and send him for a drink. As for Claire, it seemed to be her intention to dance with every alumnus in the crowd. Damaged by her second marriage, she wanted, I believe, some final contact with her 1950 contemporaries. No one enjoys being out of kilter with the times.

In the end, I had to go for my drink without assistance. Time was wasting, and all of us were getting older. Accordingly, I drank my vodka down to the grinds and then repaired to the nearest table where I was joined by Hester. She was an educated bitch and in that capacity had already tried to engross me in high-level conversation. I couldn't escape her now.

"There you are. Oh, Lee, why don't you let the lights come back on?"

Not just a bitch, she was clairvoyant, too.

"Hey," I said. "How have you been keeping these last, what, seventy years has it already been Patricia?"

"You know darn well who I am."

"Possibly. Alright, what do you want to talk about? It's getting late out there." (I pointed to out there.)

"Oh, Lee, you wouldn't believe all the things I hear about you. We're so proud for you."

(The succubus had married the town's premier roofer, an American millionaire who had permitted his wife to attend two summer sessions at L'École des Charts in Paris, France. The town gloried in her 1981 monograph on Pictish epigraphy, I believe she said.)

"Your husband, is he here?" I asked.

"Probably. But tell me about your books!"

"The books did well, but as for me, I was remaindered. I *was* lucky not to have been noticed by the critics, however. Or the masses."

We both made noises that started off sounding like actual laughter.

"Oh, Lee. Is it really true that you spent time in jail?"

She was horribly excited. I know these types, upper-middle-class provincial women still eager at age seventy-six to share in the currents of the day. She could not know that my favor was mostly for the ignorant and the poor. Or rather, that I admire only those who are continually striving and continually failing.

"I'd like to meet that husband of yours," said I. (He might not be poor, but ignorant? I never doubted it.)

"Oh, he's over there somewhere."

"Fetch him."

He proved to be pale and almost hairless and possessed a certain kind of cranial structure. He uttered words, though I was able to understand only very few of them.

"Radi sa. Polubne ra hirri!"

"Me too." We shook. He did have the hands and fingers of a roofer, not to mention that his nails were in poor condition. His right-hand thumb had no nail at all. It allowed innocent people like me to see the flesh in that hidden region before we died.

"Yuk."

"Need a new roof? We got this special stuff. Guaranteed for thirty years."

"Thirty! I'll be dead long before that."

"That's the whole idea!"

We laughed, one of us.

"Where's your house located actually?"

"No, I'm just a renter really."

"That's alright! Heck, we work for anybody."

"Oh, Tad. Lee's not just *anybody*. Be nice."

They didn't like each other very much, husband and wife.

"Shoot, we've put new roofs on half the houses in this town. Ask around, if you don't believe me."

"Oh, good Lord Tad. He believes you." And then, turning to Lee and speaking in soft voice: "He had to drop out in ninth grade you understand. But it wasn't his fault."

"We all need roofs. And besides, Plato had a much higher opinion of tradesmen and mechanics than of people like me. So do I."

Richard and Claire were still dancing, both of them bored to tears. Not that anyone could leave the floor while "The Tennessee Waltz" was playing, the one song of that era that registers on the immortality scale. In my time I have danced to that music with untold numbers of beautiful and almost-beautiful girls ensnarled in my spider-like arms. Admit it, they aren't so beautiful anymore. I wanted to cry. These girls, why on earth had they chosen to throw away the better part of what they once had been? And should be still. But never will again.

"We don't do it on purpose!" one of them claimed.

And so thus Lee, who for a good three or four minutes (a longer time than it sounds) stood looking out at a sea of women with brittle hair, congealed faces, legs in therapeutic banding. The gods were laughing.

It came to be 11:42 p.m. avoirdupois, the inside temperature standing at seventy-three degrees of mercury, and the relative humidity vacillating back and forth within a narrow ambit. Already some of the supernumeraries had left and gone home, leaving the party to stronger hands. As for those of us who had come from afar, we had taken rooms on the sixth, seventh, and eighth floors, luxurious cells with bright bedspreads and crown molding overhead. A person could draw off into his or her or their room to take a brief nap and so restore one's self. Having recessed to my own chamber, I wasted a good half-hour trying without profit to pick up the thread of a pirated edition of E. C. Large's *Advance of the Fungi*. But really, how could I concentrate when my whole past life was reenacting itself just some three stories down below? From far away came the gentle voice of Mel Tormé.

In truth, this was a luxurious building and was known to have an underground gymnasium containing all manner of weights and pulleys and other instruments. The embellishments of my own room were luxurious, too, or by my accustomed standards certainly. Available upon demand, the water was clear at first, but then began to shift from cool to warm and even further. I dithered with it, hot to warm and so on. Retrieving cold water, I quickly choked down the eleven pills and capsules assigned me by my wife. I would have expired twenty years ago without them. Or perhaps have remained a normal person. There was the picture of a goldfish pinned to the wall and just in front of it an unoccupied bowl of water. I espied a Bible in white covers with a little pot-bellied Buddha sitting on top of it. We all of us knew of course about recent legislation bearing on the equality of religions. Or the religion of equality, bad people say.

Therefore I got back into my jacket, at the same time changing over into a paisley tie that accorded with the wallpaper. I happen to be an extraordinarily good-looking man for my age, type, and intellect, on Wednesdays anyway, and this pale blue and pink cravat did nothing to vitiate the overall exhibit. Unfortunately it wasn't Wednesday, and tonight I more or less resembled a vampire without wings owing, I suppose, to the approach of midnight.

The gymnasium was located in conformity with the building's design. Except that now in addition to the weights and pulleys, it had a swimming pool in it. You can imagine my dismay to find that two of the alumni, acquaintances of mine, had taken off their shoes and some of their socks, had rolled their trousers, and were wading about gleefully in a fluid that ought have been transparent but in fact was worryingly opaque. Myself, I had rather be a professional restroom attendant than enter a pool that has been used by others. Under the diving board, I caught view of a crowd of roaches reveling over a sanitary napkin. I called to my friends, getting nothing in return. They must be drunk.

I refused to go deeper than my knees. The stuff was as cold as the Baltic, and a child's toy was drifting on the surface. Available to the public, I estimated that at least two hundred persons had urinated in these waters, and not just children either. A minute or two having passed, a longer time than it sounds, I encouraged Ralph to run upstairs and bring me a drink. If one could know all things, there would be no doubt but that some of Alexander's very piss, a molecule at least, was also adrift in this beclouded reservoir. Just then I observed an iridescent crab—I was *not* drunk—scuttling slowly toward me across the bottom. No, it was just a candy wrapper.

My drink in hand, I ascended the stairs, but then quickly came down again to get into my shoes. He refused my money, Ralph, wherefore I made a mental record to buy the man a drink of his own someday. Perhaps I *was* still drunk however, judging by my progress up the unlit staircase. I passed a decayed escrubilator, an ill-smelling thing that had sought to hide in the shadows, and then an array of posters promoting a brand of beer, car insurance, tort lawyers, female apparel, and the like. That ours might someday become a *true* country concerned with matters that actually matter, a place like Elizabethan London to offer only one example . . . You can just forget about that.

I rejoined the mob, reduced now to just a score of the more resolute invitees. I caught my first sight of Vivian, a decent human being at age twelve, now much faded. Fat, ugly, and noisy, she was transporting a tiny dog in her arms. Nor was the dog terribly appealing either. "Clarence is dead," she immediately reported, "who used to be a commercial traveler. Pancreatic problems, the papers said."

"Ha. And what was it really?"

"No, I want to talk about *you*. You come here and say things about people. Just where do you get off, acting like that?"

There was a pause. Richard was slumped against the wall, mesmerized by music and the rain. My brain rushed back to when we used to steal things from the hardware store. Other people were staring into the fire that had gone out long before, leaving behind a cask of beautifully glowing coals that looked like human faces calling out for help. So it must have been on the eve of Spotsylvania, all those soldiers foreseeing what the day might bring.

"And you don't even wear socks anymore? Wonderful."

"Really, does that seem so important to you Vivian?"

"Yes! A little bit. OK, maybe not *real* important."

"Not real important, but a little bit important?"

"That's right. Say, why do you always talk to people as if they were children Lee? That's what everybody wants to know."

"Sunspot activity. But I'll be a much nicer person tomorrow."

We both gave out with brief laughter, a wheezing noise that was far from the genuine thing. Had ever I kissed this person? Lost in the toils of preadolescent passion? On a dark rainy night? She wouldn't allow it now, and in any case her Chihuahua was growling.

"Vivian, would you care for a cup of coffee perchance?"

"Yes I would, actually."

"Good. Bring me a cup, too, would you?"

She went for it, whereon I strode quickly to the bar and fixed myself a drink with alcohol in it. The servants had mostly gone by now, though there still remained a squad of Honduran riffraff swiping off the countertops and pilfering ice cream. I looked at them severely. One was a woman, comely but black. Soon the country would belong to them entirely, and I wanted to exercise my tribe's earned benefits whilst I still could.

"Why is everybody leaving?" I asked, catching Claire by the collar as she drifted past. Instead of replying, she tore herself loose and aimed for the exit. She did still have that pertinacious nose and I had to regret that in spite of her certain resistance I had never sought to fertilize her when I still could. Came then the excrementitious Willie, who wanted to talk. I tore away from him, leaving part of my boutonniere in his unclean hand. There was an amazing number of half-finished drinks scattered among the tables, but I preferred to go to the source itself where I poured off the last of a big brown bottle of Puerto Rican rum. Richard still stood at the window, still speculating sadly at the rain. I went to him, perhaps my last opportunity for decent conversation.

"Hey! Let's go up to your cell and philosophize a bit. Want to?"

He thought about it. Only a fool would contend with me when it comes to philosophizing, wherefore I added this:

"Talk about space travel, you want to? Parallel universes?"

His room was long but narrow and hosted a bathtub large enough to contain all his wives at once. He had brought a book with him, though I wouldn't say it was anything that could have detained *my* attention. He had been drinking, Richard, and looked more like seventy-seven than seventy-six.

"Very well! Here we are. So tell me about your wives."

He groaned.

"OK, tell me about your children then. You owe me that much."

"I owe you nothing. Nor does anyone else."

"Tell me anyway."

And so he did, a sorry story relating to the quality of the late twentieth and early twenty-first centuries. Could anything be more wondrous than the decay of a country that at one time might almost have picked up where Greece left off? A "bent pyramid" that had started off in good shape.

"My daughter," he said, "was a drama major."

"Oh, shit."

"Cocaine. But they're taking good care of her! I try to visit every month."

"And what of *her* children?"

"Well, one of 'em is in Austin. I tell you Lee, we may live to see the day when HIV has been wiped off the earth! But now you're getting ready to ask about the other children aren't you? I would."

"Talk about the boys."

"Boys. Well, to start with Dion—he was the first one—he wanted to go into architecture."

"Ah?"

"But got sidetracked into candle making. He's also got him a shop where he sells old comic books to people."

"Comic book fanciers."

"Yes. And now he wants to get into beer cans, too."

"Married, is he?"

"I think so. He was at one time."

"And *his* children?"

"Right. He had a couple of 'em when he was in Nepal. Sends 'em a check *every single month*. Never misses."

"You must be proud."

"You bet. He's also a facilitator in his off-hours."

"And what does he facilitate, I wonder?"

"Positive stuff. I don't have to worry about that one anymore."

"Grandchildren?"

"I think so. We're litigating about that."

"Others?"

"Arsinoë. Turned out to be one hell-on-earth of a *progressive*. Just last month she flew to Washington to lobby for . . ."

I could feel a headache coming on. My rum was exhausted by now, wherefore I relieved Richard of the bottle he'd been husbanding for me. He was an interesting quantity, beautifully educated, but not even he had been able to stand up, like *I* had stood up, to postmodernity.

"Me, I've had just one wife, Richard," said I, "and still do. And I've loved only her since that day I first detected her striding down the lane with an odd-looking little hat bouncing up and down on her heart-shaped head." Actually I said: "My marriage, Richard, has been as nearly perfect as any that ever was."

"Lucky man."

"Indeed. And she's been lucky, too, you have to admit. Me, I'd rather be dead than be like you."

"Now you just hold it right there! You come here, insult people. Gwen was a wonderful wife. The first two years anyway."

I laughed out loud into his indeed still handsome face. With a visage like his, and given the brilliance of his flute playing, I could have fertilized every girl between Highland Avenue and Noble Street. Just then I had to wake him before he fell off to sleep in his three-piece suit.

"On the day of my marriage," I went on, "we drove for hours in the bright summer sun. I foretold the years in front of us, conscious always of my adored's eighteen-year-old profile—are you listening?—her crystalline profile staring forward with silent amazement into the kaleidoscopic future assigned to us. Ah, Richard, all my life I have wanted that she and me might be the only persons on the earth, and Time itself our joint account. Those towns, Richard, and Richard, those cities, the seas and empty buildings, they yielded at our command."

"What?"

"We have done *everything*," I said audibly, "me and she. And more still to come!"

"I'm happy for you. Getting sleepy in here, don't you think?"

"Ah, Richard. It was *Time* we wanted. And if we have neither emeralds nor three-piece suits, it's because we made far better choices than you."

"Yes, you're an admirable character. Real inspirational. A little bit tiresome maybe. But isn't it time to tell us what exactly you've contributed to life on earth?"

I backed away. He was studying me closely, like people do.

"Damn you Richard," said I. "I didn't expect that from you, I really didn't. All those years we used to steal from department stores? I don't suppose you remember that time I took up for you when Willie was fixing to . . ."

"I remember. But that doesn't give you the right to . . ."

"Sure it does."

"'The Great Lord God Almighty'—that's what Sylvia calls you."

"Oh, she does not."

"Ask her."

"What a bitch! I never was able to make any progress with that one."

"Nobody did. Well, reckon I'll turn in now."

And the person actually did remove his shoes at this time, exposing without shame a therapeutic device of some description attached to his front left foot. His shoes, unlike his feet, were of about the same size, a reminder that his father had been an esteemed podiatrist "born in the feetal position," it was said, and much respected for his work among a local ingathering of Blackfeet Indians.

The next few moments while my friend lay snoring, I was given the chance to reorganize some of his belongings. His suitcase was disappointing, a scuffed article about midway in size between a woman's handbag and other sorts of luggage much larger than that. I detest it when travelers open their equipage and permit their combs and brushes, their mouthwashes and toothpowder to form an unsteady heap atop the bed or desk. Those extra beds, seldom needed by the paying customer, have to be remade, perhaps even given fresh linens by the underpaid aborigines summoned hither on behalf of people wishing to improve the value of their shares.

To begin, I set aside the man's shaving cream, a pair of nasal scissors with blunt points, a package of

wee little batteries needed, presumably, for his pow-
ered toothbrush, and a digital reader loaded with
some high-grade journal articles touching upon tech-
nological matters. I accessed and read the first para-
graphs of a confused narration that had never been
intended for people like you or even me. Fidgeting
further with the thing, I next came upon a novel that
surprised me owing to the quality of the opening par-
agraph, quoted herewith:

> The story begins in moments from now, as soon
> as the aftermath arrives of something that hap-
> pened one time.

Wow. Not your generic twenty-first-century intro-
duction you have to admit. And yet the following lines
were better still. Having fluffed my pillow to my needs
and with regard to the hardly sufficient light, I continued on, reading deeper and deeper into that lip-
slurping English that caused all other fiction writers
to seem like amateurs. From far away I heard a train
keening through the night, a sound second only to
foghorns molested by waves, or rain upon a roof, or
parts of Wagner's *Parsifal.*

A full chapter I read, a brief experience that elevat-
ed even further my habitual cheerfulness. These
spoiled generations, surely they must pass away
someday, returning the planet to naive people living
far apart in sod-built houses. That was when Richard
came awake. I hadn't yet finished five percent of Tito's
novel.

"What the hell you doing?"

"Me? Hey, I thought we were going to talk about
science things. Parallel universes and so forth."

"It's two o'clock in the morning! Rectum!"

"Some say one thing, others another. Me, I hold with Schneider's theory."

"Schneider's an idiot. Been institutionalized, is what I hear."

"'And when you die, you can simply step off this corrupt universe and into a better one. A universe with physical laws different from ours. Or no laws at all.'"

"I'll pass."

"Of course you will. Your little three-piece suits won't do you any good over there. Your sailboats, your fifty-room houses."

"Lee?"

"Yes?"

"I really do feel like I'm about ready to fall off to sleep again. No, this time it's serious."

"You've already been sleeping!"

He reached for the lamp, but I was able without much effort to take it out of range, a shorter distance now than when he had been awake. Though I live a thousand years, never will I understand why a normal human being could opt to be unconscious when the night is dark and widespread rain is coming down in opaline drops that break into thousands of glass-like pieces on sidewalks and people's heads. I thought then of other primates sheltering 'neath canopies of leaves, highly inadequate shelters when compared to caves. No doubt the caves were taken. My thoughts turned then to the subject of wisdom and decay, the stages of. On nights like these, crimes are not being carried out at the usual level, your rapists are having second thoughts, the world is silent, and instead of people perishing slowly in office buildings, some might actually be reading.

"It's true, Richard, that we can't yet identify people in other universes. But perhaps they can identify you and me."

"I'll change my address."

"Our astronomy people are fools, Richard. They maintain our earth is perfect for the emergence of life. But that's about like saying that people are just the right size for houses and cars."

"Depends on the person."

"We'll never have the scientists we need, not till we've liberated ourselves from our East Coast graduates! Solvent people spilling over with approved opinions. We know them, you and me, right? Elite behavior soaked in egalitarian theory? They call us evil while practicing capitalism on a daily basis!"

"Just leave, okay? Please."

It was at that point that I elected to abandon the man. Like unto a sleeping snail was he, his little horns three-fourths retracted. Traveling on tiptoes, I migrated down the hall, cleaving as near as possible to the eastern wall. All the rooms were locked, leaving me no alternative but to continue forward. Here and there I discerned a wedge of light beneath a door, an indication of female dread and their everlasting fear of things lurking in the dark. That was when I recalled that rooms 304–311 had been reserved for alumni with mental impairments. I encountered Warren (a withered man, compared to what he used to be) traveling by touch along his own side of the corridor. Never had I suspected when we were young that he might someday be like me. Or rather I should say *somewhat* like me, but without the wife, integrity, intellect, and personal library. We passed without a word. My drink was almost depleted, and I saw no likely way of replenishing it at this hour.

I returned to my own cell and after disposing of some half-gallon of bodily fluid, turned down the sheets. Really, was I expected to sleep where hundreds had slept before me? Unaware that fat people had been thrashing about between these very sheets? Illegal aliens? Legal aliens? Sick people? Lepers and the AIDS infected? That some of those fat people had recently been copulating here, turning the mattress to a sponge full of semen?

Indignity is the pith of life, but that doesn't require people of my sort to endure it with equanimity. My last best hope (and all last hopes are perforce the best ones) was to relocate to one of the noble planets along with my wife; instead I switched on the television and witnessed a crime drama featuring a strong woman, a black male of high integrity, and a pusillanimous white male with a Confederate flag on the wall of his messy apartment. The following drama offered *two* strong women, each stronger than the other, both highly adept with repartee and machine guns. Gathering my courage, I switched over to a panel discussion featuring speakers from northeastern universities. One man wore a ponytail, while the woman had a pair of glassy-looking eyes that seemed to be seeking (and finding!) evidences of outright racism among the crowd.

I will admit that the bedspread looked to be new and smelled good, too. Therefore I took the thing into my arms, spread it on the floor, and after removing the (stained) pillowcase, took off most of my clothes, omitting only a few pieces of underwear. I went to the window, checked it twice, and then devoted a moment to the street down below. Normally I appreciate the granular exudations of neon lighting, particularly the greens and yellows and most of the others as well.

Developed especially for bars and taverns, this form of illumination often draws susceptible people deeper and deeper into the glowing hearts of our numerous American cities where a man can be killed, or infected, or bereft of interior organs having commercial value. Looking down into that pullulating stew, I began to feel better about myself. I know everything that can be known about human beings, for which reason I stay away from bars and neon places. You should, too. Indeed the very idea of departing this building at this hour sent me running for my pharmaceuticals.

I couldn't sleep, of course, not with so many blinking neon glyphs ricocheting off the mirror, the furniture, the lenses in my glasses, even the pages I sought to read while lying on the real hard floor. The typeface had a glossy quality typical of your better inks. All my life I have wanted to absorb information by way of a funnel inserted into that brain of mine that holds so much knowledge and beauty and hatreds piled on top of each other. And that, of course, was the moment when at the bottom of the page I blundered into a word I had never seen before, a five-syllable concoction that had caught me without my dictionary. It was rooted, that word, in Old English, with perhaps a scintilla of Latin superadded in.

I changed books, and changed locations as well, a tactic that put my nose too near the gap beneath the door. A long time had gone by since this carpet had been cleaned in any meaningful way, and I could just imagine the sort of people who had trod in this area with their unspeakable shoes. And then, too, the light was so exiguous that I had to shut my book and resort to memory for my minimum required nighttime literary intake.

"Alright, old man," said I to Lee, "it's time to get some sleep, for Christ's sakes."

And yet I remained awake. Down below I could hear a car passing by so quietly and so slowly that right away I began to worry about the sort of people on board. More realistically, I didn't really imagine they knew my name or had seen my writings. Just then my attention was drawn to the advertisements on the ceiling, a pretty girl displaying the effects of a famous toothpaste and a rhyming sonnet promoting a certain anti-freeze.

To counter all that, I tried to imagine that I was with Piłsudski on the way to Minsk. Bending over our maps in a candlelit shelter (rain coming down), we were throwing darts to choose the best deployment of our inadequate forces. On the other hand, one good Pole was worth at least one-and-a-half Bolsheviks. But it *was* odd to be dreaming about this; I hadn't done any reading in this period for a long time. Accordingly, I changed over into the captain's quarters of an eighteenth-century sailing frigate becalmed off the coast of Argentina. My oldest and most effective dream, I was soon snoring out loud, too loudly really, loud enough anyway to have angered my next-door neighbor. I arose, urinated in a cup, and poured it under his door. I had invested recently in a box of miscellaneous pharmaceuticals, the result of an end-of-business sale in my beloved hometown. Looking at myself in the mirror, I was given a disturbing but also comical reflection of the cruelties inflicted on me by the passage of time. There *are* advantages in this. No one could insist such a person behave respectably, or advance the gross domestic product, or refrain from breaking wind. The contrary indeed.

In the event, I selected a large red pill shaped (for the benefit of children, one must suppose) like a kangaroo. The jar, naturally, was ajar, and I had to probe to the bottom to retrieve the last of the colored capsules composed of I don't know what. Medicine like that ought to cure several problems all at once. Next I chose a pill with sharp corners and let it sit for a time on the tongue. According to my experience, I would soon need to visit the toilet again and thereafter might actually be able to fall off to sleep again!

Even Empedocles, who thought he was a god, had to use the toilet. And them as witnessed that, did they chuckle at the scene? Meantime the automobile four stories below had continued on its route, moving forward at perhaps five miles the hour as a little boy kept darting in and out of the thing delivering newspapers. It was the darkest part of night, but the rain itself had stopped, leaving no hint as to when we could expect it back again. In history's more advanced societies, it were raining all the time. Soon now there would be light enough for criminals to pick up where they had left off. And that green neon advertising sign? The best of the whole bunch? It hadn't survived the night.

By this time I had slept perhaps two hours, but my frigate had advanced hardly at all. My last memory was of Lee bending over a map with a decanter of brandy near at hand. I arose then, stumbled, grabbed for the curtain, and then remained standing for somewhere between two and five or six minutes while I brought myself up to present time.

The day was dark, congested with clouds, and looking out between the bars that protected my chamber, I was given an excellent view of some dozen minority members who had passed the night huddled up along the storefront in blankets or in one case a cardboard box much too small for the need. I might have tossed him a few pieces of money, but my window was pasted shut. You want a specimen of decadence? My room was under the strict jurisdiction of an air conditioner that operated nonstop whether it was wanted or not.

I found the closet, having aimed instead for the toilet. The mirror was beveled, and if I gazed at it steadily enough, I fancied I could see the melancholy images of those who had stood here before me, most of them deceased by now. I thought I could see Achilles making his way toward me through fog and smoke, his helmet lacking its plume and his shield in dreadful condition with holes in it. I saw my own adored wife beckoning me back home again.

I also used that mirror to check my teeth, pleased to see that I still had a full set. No, that had to be some other person's dentition from an earlier century, an inconstant image brought hither by this *camera obscura*, if I may denominate it so. Laughing at myself, or snorting rather in a sportsmanlike manner—I wasn't really amused—I hastened to get into my robe, the one with the tassels on it, and then stepped out into the echoing hall. Someone had left a newspaper in front of every door, one more benefit provided by a management that had also granted each tenant a pillow mint. The rent was $224.85 per night, the cost of the mint included.

Hugging the western wall, I reached the elevator and piloted it down to the main floor where, however, the auditorium was closed and locked. I decided to go to the roof.

It was chilly up there, but the stars made everything worthwhile. That green neon advertising light had come back on again, even brighter than before.

Sheltering my aging eyes (and I have never known a person whose eyes weren't aging), I found my child-hood home, a much smaller structure than it used to be. Next I located the football field where I had en-gaged in a famous and unprofitable fistfight with a boy who had died ten years ago of an illness of some sort. Usually I would come out on top in these mat-ters. I must remember to visit the varlet's grave and urinate on it.

Up here, positioned on a gravel roof with two dead pigeons on it, I was free to enjoy a cigarette without contravening the law. The smoke I produced was pe-culiarly dense and availing myself of it, I was able to reconstruct certain scenes that had transpired in this place sixty years earlier. But mostly what I saw were the faces of all those hometown girls who had chosen not to fall in love with me. One girl, living these days in New Orleans, had had the most beautiful hair, wonderful eyes, and a chin that stuck out so much that she had never married. I saw Belinda, a flaxen-headed creature who ranked at about a "6" on the town's 10-scale. (I could have lived in ecstasy on a Pa-cific atoll, provided only it had lots of girls on it.) In 1950 when we were twelve, I had taken this lovely lit-tle flute virtuoso to the movies and had held hands with her throughout, a signal event that was to domi-nate much of the gossip of the following day. No doubt the news has spread to other universes by now.

But even this was as nothing when compared and contrasted to the plague year of 1954, when the city's hospitals had been made to entertain two and some-times three persons in each separate bed. Worse still, and this finally was the very worst thing that ever happened, was the continental drift that had been saving its strength, as it seemed, to do maximum harm to my hometown. That was when my cigarette flared up brightly on account of the wind vanes at this elevation. I need hardly add that the rain had entirely petered out by now, as otherwise I wouldn't have been able to ignite the thing in the first place.

Came then voices from below where some eight or ten minority members were yelling and joking and stomping on one another. These disturbances are often made manifest when the rain shuts down and the ruck comes pouring out of their apartments. Time, meantime, was passing so slowly. I saw an enormous blackbird cruising overhead at a certain height. Would only I could have gotten myself home again by traveling all night upon its downy back!

A sudden noise. Apparently she—Gloria—had been loitering in the shadow of the chimney, also to have a smoke.

"What are you smiling about?" she inquired.

"By Jove," I emitted, "you sure did discombobulate me just now! Why are you up here on this roof where a person can view the whole town just about?"

"I was up here before you were."

I didn't pursue the argument.

"Anyway," she continued, "I wanted a cigarette."

"You've got one, it seems to me."

"No, I mean I wanted to have a smoke without getting into trouble."

"Very easy these days to get into trouble. See those minority members down there? All you got to do is say the wrong word. They carry knives longer than their members."

"What?"

"Longer than your ordinary foot ruler, or size ten shoe."

"Gosh."

"So I recommend you run on back to bed before they see you up here with that cigarette flaring in the wind."

"Say, do you remember that time we went to Tuscaloosa, and you were in the back seat with Glenda?"

The face of Glenda materialized in front of my nose. "Yes, that was one of them, the good times. Whatever happened to her, I wonder?"

"She's dead, Lee. She was in that car wreck."

"I see. Goddamn it! It never fails, *never*. Some little girl lets you kiss her, and twenty minutes later she's dead. God, I hate this system!"

"Me, too, Lee, I hate it, too. I've had these husbands, and now two of them are dead."

"Yes, rotting in their little boxes. Can't even recognize 'em anymore. Tell me, do you think Gail Russell looks like that? Andromache? Eloise? Burns me up!"

"You just have to accept it I guess."

"I accept nothing! I never have."

"Maybe that's why nobody wants . . ."

"Wants to be my friend? But you do, don't you? Friend? Truth is, I consider you the finest flute player we ever had in this town. Not that you were ever properly appreciated of course."

"Oh gosh Lee, I never played no flute!"

"But you could have."

"I was just a majorette for goodness' sakes."

"Oh yes, now I remember; you had those two big beautiful brown legs. You still have those?"

She made as if to hit me. I had seen her current partner the day before, a stalwart-looking type whose upper arm had been amputated at some date, leaving behind only a mangled forearm with tattoos on it. She said: "Look, they're opening up the bakery already!"

That was true, the same bakery where Richard and I used to invest our savings. It was my turn to speak:

"And yet, Gloria, these people, too, shall soon be dead. You must think of them as part of that minute fraction of humanity who for unknown reasons chose this time to be alive."

"There's something wrong with you Lee. I'd like to meet your wife someday."

"Ah, Gloria, Gloria, Gloria. There's an infinity of other universes out there, some of them lodged beneath your right eyelid. Out of so many possibilities, at least one of them might be rather a good place don't you think? And yet . . ." (here I paused) ". . . that's very probably what other universes believe about us!"

"They ain't nothing wrong with this world right here! I have lots of good times." (Devoid of regret, the woman simply was not living a full life. I didn't say anything, however.)

"Yes, but you deserve to be happy. Me, I've had maybe five good moments altogether, most of them before I was twelve."

"I'm not going to talk to you anymore."

And in fact she did turn and move away, leaving herself with but little time to grab off a few minutes of innocent sleep. She was to my notions the goodliest of the alumni. I could remember when the whole country had been like that.

The time came when I returned to my room, pleased that no one, as I believed, had entered during my absence. The sun, naked as a razor blade, had lifted to the horizon and was in process of carrying out its assignment, which is to say exposing the ugliness of our quotidian world. Sitting there in the last safe place available to me, i.e., the floor, I began to mull over the many problems that awaited me in Georgia, namely the lawn, the dog's left front pad, the checking account, the roof, tooth cavities, and a weight gain that was only in part countervailed by the diminution in the number of my brain cells. I bethought me then of my neighbor, and the law that wanted to take my land away. I thought about international politics and the end of antibiotics, which is not even to mention mildew in the basement and at least one scorpion known to be domiciling there. I do so hate this earthly paradigm, spores for example, rust and dust, amoebas with infectious diseases, having to work for a living. Whose idea was this? All my life I have yearned to be a spiritual substance only. For like old Mahler, "I had rather be in paradise."

As to the car, the manifold had a hole in it. The lawn? Crabgrass of course. Checking account? Weak balance, approaching subfreezing. Roof? New flashing needed. Tooth cavities? Wife one, me three. Cortex? Ruint memory.

Thus did I endure the best, or rather the worst part of an hour while dwelling on these personal concerns. Finally, after a brief nap and with the mercury moving toward 5:47 a.m., I lifted myself off the floor and mussed the bed to make it seem I'd been lying there the whole duration. I switched on the television to be cheered by an advertisement in which a likable rhinoceros was demonstrating the benefits of a brand of beer. It dismayed me how a soft drink ad had somehow attached to my suitcase while I was on the roof. What would the Greeks have said of this wondrous place—a commercial society governed by commercialists for the final victory of commerce? Recently I had become nostalgic for the Merovingians, the first people to see history as a *cyclical* process ruled by cyclical norms. I mention Chlodoburt I, and Chlodoburt II followed again by Chlodoburt I and II in strict rotation forever.

But now the time had come to consult my computer and notify myself of doings in the outside world. It's a far distance from Shanghai to my hotel, and I had to wait a long time for the electrons to cover that distance and then up the stairs to where I sat on a folded newspaper to protect me from the inseminated bed. It was broad enough, that bed, for four ordinary persons, or up to a dozen very small ones. I had wanted to learn about the revolution in Bolivia, but instead was offered four samples of unsolicited pornography of which only one deserved much attention. By analogy, I also had four messages, unsolicited also. I was being summoned to the courthouse in my Georgia hometown, the third time this information had come to me. I erased all these messages save just one, and then indulged in a hot game of online chess with a Jordanian fellow. Never ask who won.

But by now, I was thinking seriously of going downstairs for breakfast and had actually stepped out into the hall and had gone a distance before coming back for clothes. For this last day, I had chosen the best clothes in my possession, namely an Italian suit that not so long ago had actually fit my person. My shoes were Italian, too, made, one might almost think, of the pelts of unborn hummingbirds. (Owing to the inequality of my two feet, I had had to acquire two pair in order to form one usable combination. [I still hope someday to find a buyer for the ones left over.]) I mention, too, my hi-tech watch, a fluorescent product with special properties. Manufactured under license from the C.I.A., the thing includes an interrogation device duplicitously called a "barometer."

I have so many beautiful ties (most of them from the Balkan region) that gladly would I have worn six or seven of them at the same time. In the end, I selected a blue paisley that I intend eventually to bequeath to the Brent Museum of Nonrepresentational Art. It was such a sinuous thing, hand-painted, and pricey; I keep it in the depths of my closet. My socks were paisley, too, and never mind the prejudice, the bias, the discrimination, and the bigotry they seemed to incite. These, too, had formed a pair at some date, before an inadvertent separation had sent the best one somewhere else. As for my garters, those that had come down to me from my Confederate ancestor, I wore them as proudly as a flower. Finally, happy with myself, I stood back and tried out various facial expressions to go with my clothes.

I entered the restaurant, the first of all the alumni, and took a place by the window whence I might keep an eye upon the impending day. The waitress was a representative of what happens to lower-class white people whose husbands and offspring have gone away and left them without so much as a recycled postcard at Christmas time. This one was past being surprised by anything and had long before reconciled with life's upside-down value system. You don't want to be a generous person, much less an unpretentious one in a world like this.

I smiled at her, a painful operation for a person of my type, and then submitted an order for the usual eggs, grits, sprats, coffee, and jelly. The silverware was heavy, the way I like it, and bore the crest of the Podalski Cutleries of Podalski, North Dakota. And yet, the forks had just three tines instead of four, one more specimen of the profiteering mindset of the upper Midwest. I prefer *unabbreviated* silverware, and insist that at all times my egg yolks be unbroken and the vitellus the proper shade of sunset gold. I ordered some other things, too, and demanded that the unutterable music be brought to a stop. This left me with perhaps ten minutes of uninterrupted thinking.

Setting free my facial expression, I thought rapidly for about five minutes, finishing up with one of the best cups of coffee I had had since leaving home. I smiled in the direction of the waitress, alarming her unnecessarily. Entered then the appalling Willie. I hid my face, unaware at first that he was carefully ignoring *me*. I saw others, children of the emerging generation, a normal group by current standards. Bland, cheerful, optimistic, I *know* these people, predestined as they are to give consideration to two or three easily available philosophies and then to clasp one of them forever to their breasts.

"Ah, me," said I. "Life has ended. And I the last true man on earth!"

I refused to cry, ordering instead another cup of that good coffee that justified itself by the way it colluded with the cream. But all this quickly fell out of mind when I was served two fried eggs with perfect blisters, a scoop of excellent grits with true butter, three sticks of bacon, and a slice of cantaloupe. That was when a forty or maybe fifty-year-old girl began asking, courteously enough I suppose, if she could share my table. I had completed the eggs but the bacon had shattered into fragments too small to lift save on the tip of a person's tongue. Next came Beverly, a great beauty at one time, who sat down beside me.

"Hello, Lee," she offered. "You're looking kind of . . ."

"Yes, I know. You, on the other hand . . ."

"Let's not even talk about it, agreed?"

We made that compact. Truth was, she didn't look so terribly bad, considering her disorganized history.

"You going to eat that bacon?"

I gave it over to her. Were you to stare uninterruptedly at that person for a minute or two, you might begin to recapitulate the pretty girl she once had been.

"How come you never went out with me?" I asked.

"You never asked!"

"And if I had?"

"Pass the salt please. If you will."

All unawares, a roach had alit upon her sleeve. (It was of course the woman, not the insect, who was unaware. We still know almost nothing about the mental processes of these creatures. Nor of insects either.) We looked at each other, the roach and I. I yearned to slay the thing, had only I been able to do so without besmirching the woman's blouse.

I had expected Richard to join us, but that was before he spotted Beverly sitting just next to me. There was some blood between those two, something to do with a bit of cruelty, as Beverly saw it, concerning her long-deceased cat. Meantime, Richard had ordered a boiled crustacean of some description, a half-dead creature with its mouth all agape. I watched with horror as my former friend consumed the wretched thing. It's so disgusting, food is, and the demand for it gives proof of humanity's hopeless prospect for spiritual improvement.

"Still married?" I inquired of Beverly. "To that same fellow?"

I had to wait till she swallowed.

"Oh, yes. You?"

"No, I married someone else."

She laughed. I had spent full six months in 1950 trying in vain just to make her smile.

"Is that her?"

"No, no, that one just came and sat down. She did ask, however."

"I think she's listening to us."

"You bet your ass she's listening! Wouldn't you?"

"Oh, I suppose. You put ketchup on your eggs?"

"No, actually my nose is bleeding."

She laughed. Someday I hope to recount these witticisms in full. She had been famous in her youth, had Beverly, for her *three separate teethings*, each new growth preempting the previous one. Unhappily, her nose continued to veer off to one side.

"They could fix that now," I said. "Modern medicine."

"Thanks for that Lee."

(She wasn't really that bad.)

"Maybe if you just took real short breaths and held 'em for a while . . ."

"Oh, Christ. You'll never change."

"Hell, I could take you upstairs this very moment and give you more pleasure than you ever . . ."

"So long, sweetie."

She left. I had had almost four cups of coffee by this time, each following cup a little less enjoyable as I for my part grew less susceptible to the effects. There were by now a score or more of sleepy-looking alumni in the room, all of them looking off into the distance as they grudgingly came awake. I had slept less than any of them, and probably less than all of them together. But mine was far the most beautiful of the ties. And my weathered face looked more than ever like a tapped-out writer's.

I gathered my newspaper and made an attempt to
read it. Sad, how modern information is offered in
such tiny script readable only by the young, who have
small need of it. The uninvited one had chosen to
stay.

"What, y'all having some kind of meeting or something?"

"No, we're like, you know, just chilling. You feel
me?" Suddenly I exclaimed out loud: "Oh, look at this!
Congress is allowing a fifteen percent tax rebate for
people who marry opposite races!"

"Who was that woman?" (She was pointing at Beverly.) "Is that your wife?"

Well, I had to laugh at that. That woman, so-
called, wasn't good enough to bake cookies for my
divine one's manicurist. "No," I said aloud, "that was
just Beverly. A good person though."

"What's the story with her nose?"

I left. There were other tables and other alumni,
other grits and manifold half-filled coffee pots. It
wasn't till too late that I saw I had seated myself just
next to Lloyd. I hadn't thought about him for years
and wouldn't have guessed that he still existed.

"Lloyd!" I said.

"Hey! Say, I'd forgotten about you!"

"And why shouldn't you, for example? I was pretty
much a colorless person back then."

"Still is," came a voice from somewhere.

"Colorless. Yeah, I remember now. How you been
making out?"

"How does anyone make out these days, trying to
survive in a land of the most extreme decadence? We
were warned, you have to admit, by Spengler and Nietzsche, and those boys."

He didn't hear me, Lloyd did not. Still suffering from last night's alcohol, he had let his rather featureless face come to rest in the remains of his cantaloupe, where it made a perfect fit. This is what my generation had come to. Even so, I offered my napkin to the churl, who used it to blow his nose. I was still being followed by that uninvited woman, a younger sort of type entranced by the behavior, the appearance, the follies, and the plain simple aplomb of her elders.

"Oh, yeah!" Lloyd said suddenly. "*Now* I remember you! You're Floyd!"

We had to laugh. "No, no." (More laughter.) "Floyd's your brother!"

"Right."

I called for further coffee, which was fetched to me by a slim-hipped hippy in odd-looking glasses. Speaking quietly, but not quietly enough, she referred to my coffee addiction: "Good. Maybe now you'll drown."

All my life I have wanted to seize upon such people and do things to them. I still dream of lifting out this one's eyes with a spoon and returning them to the wrong sockets. Instead, I merely glared at her with a gaze fortified by my age and experience, my readings and integrity and the rest.

"You're Jimmy then?" Lloyd asked. His face was sincere.

"No, no, no. My name is Lee!"

"I doubt it. No, I remember ole Lee. He was the one who used to . . ."

I stopped him just in time. He had aged even more rapidly than me, and no doubt had saved up all sorts of true and untrue rubbish in his head. Returning to my newspaper, I sought to find one of my favorite all-time cartoon characters, a stone-age individual wont to drive back and forth on a user-friendly dinosaur. Really, I need to keep score on all the good things the modern age ignores. Where is Dagwood, and where Kathryn Grayson? Where the skating rink and where the lake where my father caught a seventeen-pound bass? Where the old Ford car that used to go clack, clack, clack on Highway 43 all the way to Panama City? Bend with the breeze they say. No, though I be dead, someday the breeze will bend for *me*. Truth is— and I feel about seventy percent sure of this—the Godhead loves people like me.

"I stand against the tide."

"Right!" Lloyd said. "Fuck 'em in the teeth!"

I noticed then that Richard was standing some distance away whispering confidentially to a reasonably well-preserved woman who looked faintly like a girl I used to know. Neither of these people had entirely given up on life, and both had been fitted with plausible wigs. He was a charming person still, was Richard, and now once again was using his high school football experience for discussion material. Determined to be free of my tablemate, I rose, stretched, yawned, and then dashed over to Richard and with some considerable difficulty made a place for myself between the girl and him.

"Don't believe him," I said. "I doubt he played more than fifteen minutes the whole season. And fumbled twice."

"Once. I fumbled once, for Pete's sake. And anyway we were twenty-one points ahead, and so it didn't matter."

"Didn't matter, my rear end! And you wonder why the coach never put you back in again?" And then turning to the girl: "The coach never put him back in again."

"He was doing his best!" said the uninvited teenage guest.

"Yes. That's the tragedy of it."

Meantime out on the floor, the minstrel show was continuing and had come to that place where two blackamoors were arguing over the division of a watermelon. Of course we were amused, all of us, and could only wish the world were still that way, when a decent shoeshine could be had for two bits or less. We were still chuckling over the comedy when the toast-master dissolved the performance and brought the curtain down. Followed then a not very gifted stand-up comedian offering jokes about body parts and the products of human elimination. He didn't comprehend that we had finished that stage of life and would have preferred something a little less undignified, so to speak. It embarrassed me, I admit it, to be the last one laughing.

It was 9:17 (a.m.) on a wet October day in northeast Alabama, the choicest part of the South's noblest state. Affected by the weather, I returned to my room, micturated, and then continued there as I turned over several thoughts in my head. In the meantime the maids had (unnecessarily) remade the bed, leaving another mint candy on the pillow. I accepted it, consumed it, and left a dime in its place. No use to try for sleep, not with two or three thoughts still running up and down inside my beehive head. Rather than sleep, I changed over into another tie, this one a pink artifact bought online from London, home of some of the best ties this side of Pakistan. It was too gaudy for a person of my age, of course it was, and yet . . .

Ten

. . . I wore it anyway.

But by now the alumni were leaving town. I saw an old woman, formerly a flute player, carrying a clothing bag large enough for my divine's whole wardrobe. Really, what is it between women and clothes? Ties I can understand.

The time had come for displaying photographs of one's descendants and decedents, hundreds of pictures posted for easy viewing on three walls. They all looked alike to me, save for the Mongoloid. Worse yet, these children and grandchildren were accompanied more often than not with a brief description—I wanted to puke—of the person's achievements, and in one case a few lines of distasteful poetry. I studied those faces in detail, hoping to find somewhere an aspirational sort of person, which is to say a man of parts, literate and wise, full of hard-won integrity. A courageous type, about six feet tall let us say, who in youth had been good alike at tennis and chess. Who had yearned not for money but for Time, and yearned for it still. But what I found, of course, was row upon row of fungible types: pulmonary specialists, roofers, government thralls, retired military, three realtors with slits for eyes, four accountants (one of them merely a bookkeeper), claims adjusters, a skin job, a webpage designer, the part-owner of a hardware store, a crash test volunteer, six tax preparers, a professional suntan model, and four college professors in possession of the array's most startling visages. Had any of these striven to compose operas or climb the Matterhorn? Had any dreamt of becoming a high-wire acrobat, or cattle rustler, or even just a decent counterfeiter with wads of cash? Don't ask. No, the age of interesting employment ended at about the time my grandfather's brick mill shut down. Thankfully, Richard hadn't abandoned me yet.

"Bring me a drink will you?" I reasoned. "A Tom Collins for example."

"You've turned into a damn sot Lee."

"I have not. I only drink when the stuff is free."

"Blackguard, is what you are. What were you talking about with Beverly?"

"About you. But she's a good person, Rich, and didn't actually use your name."

"White of her. Oh say, do you remember when we used to steal stuff from Woolworth's? And when we turned old man Weaver's flowerpots upside down?"

"I remember you stealing and me trying to stop you."

"*Drole.* And that time you peeped in Belinda's window?"

"I remember me peeping and you trying to stop me."

"I waddn't even there!"

"Should have been."

"Look, people are leaving. Who is that one, for Christ's sakes?"

"Arleen."

"Died years ago."

"You don't think she'd miss reunion do you?"

In the end, he fetched me coffee, but with a deal too much cream in it. Considering the person he is, he absolutely refused to fetch another. That was when Phillipina cut across my view. Owing to her outfit, I could not immediately find if she still possessed those two gibbous and almost indistinguishable buttocks known among the townsfolk as Uranus and Neptune.

"She was twelve years old!"

He was right. No doubt I had been thinking of one
of the high school girls.

"Well, who was Uranus and Neptune then?"

"And remember when we used to gather at the
skating rink and torment those people?" (My friend
had been loitering up North for the last several years
and had come away with one of those preposterous
accents.)

"Yes, I do. Out on Glenwood you mean?"

"No, no, no. Across from the Last Chance Taber-
nacle."

"Oh, right! Say, maybe we ought to pay them another little visit, if you know what I mean."

"Except that no one goes skating anymore."

My undisciplined mind reverted to the music and
all those skeletons now circumnavigating the floor on
metal wheels. We had moved, Richard and myself,
into the little alcove at the further end where the ush-
er was less likely to tell us that we had used up our
rent and really ought to leave. Here we could avail us
of our tobacco habits with little fear of being arrested.

"Those were the days."

"Yes. But just wait till the reaction sets in. Though
we be dead, yet our day will come."

"'Our day will come.' Isn't that what Faulkner said?"

"No, that was Céline said that."

"He said your day will come?"

"He said his own day will come! Not mine."

"Damn right, your day ain't coming. I have to agree
with the man."

"It will come, my day, before your day has even
thought about coming!"

"Not in a billion years."

"I can be patient."

"No, Lee. First, we must have a catastrophe of some kind."

"A really big one do you say, or just a garden-variety sort of thing?"

"Big, very big."

"Sounds good to me. One acre of fertile ground, that's all a good man needs to support his family. And maybe a cow."

"One acre. Is that like, say, the size of a football field? I'm not good with acres, the size of."

And:

"Make a revolution, Richard, or else have nothing to do with people."

"Revolution is hard."

"Be invisible then. And do nothing that can be viewed on cathode ray tubes."

(I couldn't have said which of us held the floor, we spoke so rapidly.)

It was almost five o'clock by now and we two the last remaining survivors of our epoch and kind. I had caught the registrar looking in our direction and tried to read his lips as he spoke into his telephone, an instrument of proven convenience that allows people to communicate with each other over distances.

"Hmm," said I. "He's called the police. I suppose they'll be coming for us now."

"And force us out into the cold wet rain?"

"Yes. That's how people like us are treated these days."

"Drunk people, you mean?"

"Exactly."

In the parking lot I saw a gathering of toads carrying out a reunion of their own. Saw, too, the same scarlet bird I had seen the day before when the thing was still alive. An artifact as beautiful as that never had a chance in postmodern times. And now, owing to the deluge, the very fireflies had retreated to their hives. But I was not unhappy. His cigarettes, Richard's, had good flavor, and I had the prospect of driving back to Georgia through my favorite kind of weather.

Eleven

I ran the whole distance to the car, minimizing my exposure to some two score of migrants congregated at the corner. Of course I still had miles to go, or one mile at least before breaking out into the outlying countryside where I could put my DeSoto to the test. I have always trusted in the kindness of my car. I plunged across the intersection, ignoring the light which in any case happened to favor me. I saw an old man drifting down the sidewalk at this hour, entirely vulnerable to the undocumented but highly motivated workers waiting sixty yards further down. (Old man? He was younger than me, for Christ's sakes!) I saw two girls who either were whores or else devoted to present-day couture. I passed a suntan salon, a saloon, a salsa factory, a soap manufacturer, and other evidences of our strong economy. Came next a controversial movie with a long line of old men pushing and shoving to get out of the rain. (Old men? See above.) And then, finally, the African slum just east of town. I have seen better-organized and more aesthetic spaces around used-car lots, or in lithographs of famous battle scenes. A dead dog lay in the gutter, its intestines damming up a pool of rainwater perfect for larvae. A garbage can lay upside down, revealing a contents composed of half-eaten meals, hypodermic needles, used ammunition, and a fetus in a jar. And in short it was a district, I would have said, where the space-time coordinates had fallen out of kilter.

The open highway! But I still had three blocks to go. The day was almost dark, and yet large clusters of Bell Curve types were still at large. All I have ever wanted was a parallel road system reserved for Lee alone. As mentioned above, I do admit to a certain liking for downtown neon, a granular stuff that brings tears to those as know how to appreciate the same. But nothing could resonate as much with me as *cold blue lights seen from far away*, mysterious signals pointing out the location of unearthly things.

I could have traveled faster but for the incredible mess from those new-style passenger toilets made optional this year in higher-priced automobiles. Could have gone faster had not I fallen behind a truck—the driver was grinning—who refused to let me pass. By habit I reached for my .357 Magnum eight-shot Smith and Wesson before thinking better of it and returning the gun to its place, never mind exactly where. The weapon was heavy, an anti-accelerant that prevented the car from attaining its best speeds. Other burdens included a significant weight of cultural equipment, three volumes from the *Oxford English Dictionary* for example, a ballpoint pen with auxiliary ink, a gazetteer of Pangaea, and one recently unpackaged quire of #24 high-fiber-content foolscap writing paper.

Came 7:27 in the dark, I veered off to the right. I knew enough about this route to avoid the towns and cities or any location indeed with more than a thousand inhabitants. Someday, I like to dream, the whole world will have no more than that. But hadn't gone more than a few hundred yards before I caught sight of a bedraggled youth trying to flag down a ride. He was tired, judging from him, and was actually sitting on the asphalt with his thumb up in the air. His dog was just as exhausted; his two long ears touched the ground and folded back on themselves. A hitchhiker myself at one time, I slowed and pulled over, welcoming the dog with a pat and then accelerating in order to outrun the man. I have always trusted in my DeSoto automobile, a rebuilt device with lots of miles left in her still.

My intention was to get me home again before the brash sun should come and illumine every bad thing within a certain perimeter. Another intention of mine was to drive forward steadily, looking straight ahead as the miles slipped by; instead, there suddenly appeared a barrier, or "gate" rather, that blocked progress until travelers had correctly answered at least seven of ten questions regarding the advantages of a certain operating system for home computers. I had been traveling at 45–52 miles per hour, a tempo that sorted well with the Abravanel version of Mahler's Eighth Symphony just then playing on the machine. The dog seemed to like it, too. Passed thus some half-dozen miles when I caught sight of one of the best things in days, a down-and-out roadside restaurant still doing business at 9:07 in the late afternoon.

It was dimly lit, my first requirement of such places, and had an assemblage of some thirty or forty cars and trucks (including motorcycles and tractors) parked at odd angles around the structure. I pulled over, stopped, and, putting the car in reverse, came back and parked between a corroded truck with a patriotic bumper sticker and a Hungarian sports car with a load of electronic equipment in the rear. Or mayhap plumbing supplies, for as much as I could confidently say. I was old, old and corroded, but I knew that in this region of Alabama well-dressed elders are usually given the respect we deserve. And I was willing to take my fourth meal of the day in order to inspect the interior of this down-and-out establishment and its clientele.

As foreseen, the place was dimly lit, and those sought by the police (as I reckoned them to be) had drawn off into the four corners where only the tip of someone's nose or a tankard of beer could intermittently be seen. I was greeted with a low murmur of approval followed by enduring indifference. I was a white man and much too old to comprise a danger to anyone. Wearing a spiritual face, I doddered to a place that lay over against a salad bar offering browned lettuce and pork rinds and not much else. Climbing slowly into my glasses, I verified that the menu, though brief, had been updated in pencil. I perceived the scent of coffee and barbecue coming from some area of this authentic if also rather higgledy-piggledy place with worn-out linoleum on the floor and campaign posters for General MacArthur on the wall. Except when sleeping in the arms of my woman, I am never more comfortable than when in places just like this.

As to the tiny waitress, I watched her hurrying back and forth in her apron and canvas footwear. Life somehow just hadn't worked out for her. Divorced twice, she had now come to the age of, say, fifty-one or two and suffered from migraines, varicose veins, and three children, one of them dead and the others far away. A prototype of her special kind, why really had this conspicuously unprepared person been condemned to life in the first place? I was moved, I admit it, mostly on account of the thinness of her legs and the baffled expression on her face. Someone has to be

swindled that someone else may own a mansion—
everyone knows that. But oh my goodness, I do so
hate that system!

I called her to my table and right away began the
interrogation.

"Could I have the barbecue with some of that real
good sauce on it?"

She wrote it down with an amputated pencil that
sorted with her stature.

"My son," said I—(I have no sons)—"just loves the
way you folks do your barbecuing! How about you—
you have any sons?"

I needed a minute to cajole, or command her rather, to seat herself across from me.

"Was it meth?" I asked, regarding her son.

"I reckon. He didn't talk about it much, you understand. He was a real good ball player though. When
he was in high school."

"No doubt about that. Was he married?"

"Oh, sure. Married that rotten . . . Oh, he was married alright."

"She's probably the one that got him into so much
trouble."

"You're right about that! I warned him. But you
might as well talk to a brick wall!"

"She'll get her reward. When the time comes."

"Don't you just know it. It wouldn't bother me if it
came tomorrow!"

"Or yesterday."

We laughed. Not loudly and not extendedly, but
we did laugh.

"It's the children I worry about," I testified.

"You got that right. He's turning out just like his
father! Jimbo, I mean."

"And the others?"

"Gwen might be alright. Looks like me, everybody says."

"She'll do fine."

(When was the last time you had a conversation like this in the goddamn North?)

"I wanted her to go to colledge."

"Certainly. You just about have to go to colledge these days if you expect to . . ." (Salary, social position, etc., etc.)

I hit the highway at a little past ten. The road was like a hoard of jewels, owing to the car lights and advertisements and here and there a surviving firefly left over from better days. Nights, rather. I hewed to that discontinuous yellow stripe that runs down the center of roads like a succession of arrows coming straight toward me. Even so, I was making good time and still had three, four, maybe five gallons of medium-grade gasoline sloshing about in the purported fuel tank that I have never actually seen. But of course the same could be said for gears and hard drives and a number of other things on which a modern person perforce depends.

As reported, I was traveling at a decent speed when a logging truck filled to the gunnels with loblolly pine came up behind and began tooting at me to travel faster.

"I'm going as fast as I can!" I yelled back, forgetting that he couldn't hear. "He"? In fact he was a woman behind the wheel, another displaced person carrying on an activity intended for men. I could feel my gorge rising. My revolver was out of easy reach, however, and anyway I couldn't say with certainty what quality of person she might have been. An abandoned woman with children or a more modern type with a great many tattoos running down her spine? In the event, I elected to continue driving forward not one whit faster than I could. Meantime, far above, I had brought into focus a ragged cloud that in this unique case didn't seem to resemble anything to compare it to. No doubt about it, winter was coming in, that annual crisis that is so hard upon old people with thin blankets and astounding heating bills. That was when the driver behind me swerved abruptly and came hurrying forward, as if she imagined I'd let her get in front of me.

I crawled to the next town where at last the woman was thrown off course by stop signs and traffic lights and her own poor instinct with time-space assessments. The store I wanted, or anyway the one I found, was wedged between an all-night ice cream parlor and a vacant lot where some one or two persons of Mayan appearance had built a fire. I greatly admire these migrants, fruit-pickers and the like, who had bravely chosen to abandon their own countries simply in order to share in an economy that they themselves couldn't have created in a thousand years. In truth, I adore the whole of humanity, martyrs, geniuses, and heroes, members of this most supernal of the species.

I chose my store at an intersection cluttered with enough fast food outlets to have sustained the army of Xerxes for months on end. Proceeding with caution, I parked in the authorized place and was about to leave the vehicle when I observed that the adjacent car contained a dog of its own, a mixed species, anxiety-ridden. Recognizing each other for what they were, the two dogs, that one and mine (mine was still licking the barbecue sauce from his two thin lips), began expostulating happily across the eighteen inches that kept them apart. What the hell. The window was down, and I chose without much delay to exchange my animal for the adjacent one.

The time was almost ten thirty when I stepped into the store and with the arrogance intrinsic to people of my type, strode past the cashier. Bored to tears, cloudy ones running down his nearside cheek, the man was watching a basketball game on an enormous television set that stood in lieu of all those books he hadn't read. I have no patience with people. Even so, I smiled sweetly at him and then proceeded directly to the rear of the store where there seemed to be a hoard of unsold and outdated tools and carpentry equipment, some of them inexplicable to city persons and me. One need only to pick up those things one by one and turn them over to see what time had done, namely to make life easier, requiring less skill and manly exertion, the chief requirements of today's decadence. On what grounds need we have respect for hardworking people who no longer work very hard? Today there exists an implement that drives nails by gas pressure, for God's sakes. At one time, a hand drill operated like an eggbeater; now it looks more like a hairdryer. Goggles are worn, as if people were no longer willing to risk even just one, and that one a surplus, of their precious eyes.

All my life I have said and continue at intervals to say even today that American society has become but a lower-case recapitulation in miniature of what has already been done in Europe. Music? Philosophy? Better had the job been given to the Maori.

I headed toward the nails and screws, remembering how in more authentic times wooden pegs were used. I do admit that these newer articles are more uniform in size, less inclined to rot, and require less artistry. The store did supply a cute little shovel by aid of which the customer could scoop up wanted items and dump them in a brown paper bag. I bought a half pound of #6 nails, enough to justify my visit. Continuing on, I invested in a bottle of aloe that bore an attractive label, and then a Chinese-produced putty knife bearing hieroglyphs of that ludicrous script.

Beyond that, I bought nothing else, excepting only a tube of glue needed for rebinding old books. I bought a flashlight that held three batteries, a jar of assorted nuts and bolts, an alkaline car wax for my DeSoto, a box of .357 Magnum barbed cartridges, and a baseball cap with the Confederate flag on the bill. In times to come, such items might be as requisite as food and water and Internet connections.

I bought some other things as well, but rather than listing them it were better to pick up with the events that took place after I had dealt with the proprietor. A thin person, astigmatic, liverish, and atrabilious to a degree, he was a fair example of what happens to people.

"Ahoy!" I said with good cheer. "Still raining outside."

"Pretty obvious."

"You sure do have some interesting things in here. Old tools. Comb honey in a box. Reminds me of . . ."

He held up his hand to stop me.

"Forty thousand, and I'll sign it over to you. The whole goddamn kit and caboodle."

"Forty?"

"That's right. Taxes. I'm losing money even as you stand over there by all those discounted things."

"And plumbing supplies?"

"That, too."

"I'm retired actually."

"Perfect! When you got a business like this one, you'll have even more free time. OK, how about thirty-seven and a half?"

"Whew. How much taxes do you owe actually?"

"And I'll throw in that old Chevy outside, too. You can't do better than that. Nobody can."

I needed to think. The shop was stocked with automobile parts, including a hood ornament of a woman with a superior physique. It's true that I did possess a solid sixteen thousand dollars altogether, some in gold and some in coin and some, twenty-two dollars, in my billfold.

"Five thousand," I offered.

"What did you say just now? Sounded like 'five.'"

"Agreed?"

"Goddamn son-of-a-bitch! And I thought you was a good person!"

"I was."

"Go on, get the fuck out of here, goddamn stinking whoreson, get out before I . . . !"

Again I held up my hand to stop him.

"OK, I'm leaving. See? I'm opening the door, even though it was largely open already. And now you can think of me as having never even been here!"

(It was the first time in a long time that I had gotten away without paying.)

The open highway! But first I had to go back a few hundred roads and correct the choice that I had made *where three roads run together*, a site very like that infamous intersection where Oedipus had slain his father. All my life I have chosen the route "less traveled by," a famous cliché familiar to readers of that line. In the event, I selected the way that *wasn't* a mistake, and then proceeded at top speed to leave the state where, according to the song, a great many jag-

ged stars had fallen the previous night. More seriously, I really was drawing nigh to well-regarded Georgia,
the best place in the world that happens at the same
time to be my own home state.

Twelve

I will say it again, that the highway by night looked
like a capsized box of jaspers and amethysts and the
disembodied eyes of wild animals. I came to a succession of tiny signs posted about fifteen feet apart offering lines of poetry on behalf of a shaving cream that I
for my part now promised to patronize. Not all good
things had vanished, not yet. I saw a distant city going
up in flames, an entrancing sight that came into focus
just as the fourth movement of tonight's symphony
was getting under way. I imagined I were a boy again,
again speeding toward my grandmother's enormous
home with its twenty-foot ceilings, its frosted glass
windows and china cabinet, and the woman herself
waiting in her apron amid her gingerbread and pies. A
bed (built by her husband) awaited me there, not to
mention the washstand whereon there used to stand a
highly articulated porcelain pitcher full of cold water
lifted by hand from the complicated geology that un-
dergirds the town. I stopped. It wasn't as if I didn't
already abominate modernity enough that I need re-
mind myself the reasons thereof. After all, everyone
knows what has been gained, leaving only just me to
record what has been forgot.

Georgia, you may know, was organized in the sev-
enteenth century out of a number of topographical
counties labeled with mile-high lettering that runs
across the various terrains. Automobiles try to avoid

these things lest they end up as a "typographic error," as those of us call it. This explains one, but by no means all, of the reasons I carry a sleeping bag in my old car, as also four days of rations in aluminum foil.

Thirteen

So it was that by 11:17 I was back on the road again, slicing deeper and deeper into occidental Georgia in the dark black night. I wanted to be home already, *now*, instantaneously; instead, I had far to go in order to arrive there. This is the sort of thing that causes me to be so bitter, this and appendicitis, rust, change, humidity, and the tendency of books to topple over onto one side. Off to the right, I espied the ruins of a gristmill that had fallen to ground, a dilapidated vision that revealed nothing of the love affairs that had originated there. No one had written them down, and no doubt those people have expired by now. Myself, I just wanted to be in the arms of my wife but wasn't. Why? These are the irritants that have ruined my life.

ABOUT THE AUTHOR

Tito Perdue was born in 1938 in Chile, the son of an electrical engineer from Alabama. The family returned to Alabama in 1941, where Tito graduated from the Indian Springs School, a private academy near Birmingham, in 1956. He then attended Antioch College in Ohio for a year, before being expelled for cohabitating with a female student, Judy Clark. In 1957, they were married, and remain so today. He graduated from the University of Texas in 1961, and spent some time working in New York City, an experience which garnered him his life-long hatred of urban life. After holding positions at various university libraries, Tito has devoted himself full-time to writing since 1983.

His first novel, 1991's *Lee*, received favorable reviews in *The New York Times*, *The Los Angeles Reader*, and *The New England Review of Books*. Since then, he has published thirteen other novels—including *The New Austerities* (1994), *Opportunities in Alabama Agriculture* (1994), *The Sweet-Scented Manuscript* (2004), *Fields of Asphodel* (2007), *The Node* (2011), *Morning Crafts* (2013), *Reuben* (2014), the *William's House* quartet (2016), *Cynosura* (2017), and *Philip* (2017)—which have been praised in *Chronicles: A Magazine of American Culture*, *The Quarterly Review*, *The Occidental Observer*, and at *Counter-Currents*.

In 2015, he received the H. P. Lovecraft Prize for Literature.

www.ingramcontent.com/pod-product-compliance
Lightning Source LLC
Chambersburg PA
CBHW021337290326
41933CB00038B/878